One Girl's Army

One Girl's Army

Chloe Ormerod

To order additional copies of this book, contact:
Xlibris
800-056-3182
www.Xlibrispublishing.co.uk
Orders@Xlibrispublishing.co.uk
775086

Contents

Chapter 1

Childhood Nightmares

Scarlet's Childhood Fears

Some say you can dream what you want to be in this world. But others say it takes more than just luck to get to that dream. All the hard work, mistakes, and complications you have to go through can push you further and further away from your dream and make you want to give up. You might start to think you'll never be like your idols, standing on a podium and embracing the light of your successes.

For twenty years, I knew what that felt like. All I wanted was to live a normal life. But what is normal about life when you're fighting to survive while at war or when you were put in state care and watched your family sacrifice themselves for you or when the one you love betrays you because he or she doesn't have the nerve to step up for you?

Fear can manipulate your mind and torture your emotions and even drive you to insanity. But that's a coward's way of looking at challenges. Going completely insane because of a fear is what would really be insane. As long as you can carry on, it doesn't matter how scared or desperate you are.

You are taught to fight through difficult and painful times, to be strong against bullies, and to no longer be the victims society has always portrayed you as. Everyone can be strong, rather than being the typical underdog who thinks him or herself no good at anything. That was me when I was younger.

They once called me the weak one, not considering what I'd been through. Luckily, friends and a family member I'd never met before were always there for me while I went through a mental breakdown that almost caused me to commit suicide. I couldn't face the fact that I was alone. My older brother, Nathaniel, had given his life to save mine, rescuing me from a well at the children's home we'd been sent to. Through most of my childhood, I had isolated myself from others because I thought it was my fault Nathaniel had died.

My foster parents, the care workers at the children's home, and even some of the kids told me it wasn't my fault. Now, looking back at those memories, I realise they were right. But if they were in my position, they would have felt the same way.

I was only seven years old the day my brother and I were about to be fostered. I was playing with some of the girls at the care home in the tree house when I slipped on a branch and fell into the wishing well. That's when I learned what it feels like to have the only family by your side—my older brother—sacrifice himself for you. The memory still makes my heart sore.

Nightmares have haunted me since that day. They show me what would have happened if it were me who had died or provide other alternative scenarios. Eventually, everything turns to darkness—the one fear I still possess.

Darkness controls my dreams, transforming them into nightmares that make me feel unsafe to sleep and cause insomnia. They tear open the wounds of my past and make them bleed from the fear that still dwells in the back of my mind.

Scarlet Comes Face-to-Face with the Mistress of Darkness

The first time I feared darkness was when I was ten years old, three years after Nathaniel died. I was being cared for by my foster parents, the Fendersons—George and Nicole. They had three children of their own. Conner, their oldest, was a senior in high school. Jodie was in the middle of her third year of high school. And last but not least was their youngest son, Toby. He and I were the same age, and he understood me and my fear of the dark.

When he heard someone else had the same fear, Toby felt like he wasn't alone. Instead of his parents, brother, and sister to comfort him, he finally had someone to talk with about it. Toby believed a shadowy beast lurked in every corner when darkness flooded the room. Even a little bit of light cast shadows of terrifying figures that watched his every move as he peeked out from under his quilt. Sometimes he thought the shadows were moving around, stalking him through the darkness. According to Toby, when his parents, Jodie, or Conner woke up, they were like the light, making the shadows disappear and making him feel safe.

For me, the darkness lurked in my nightmares. It was in the darkness during that period of time when I first laid eyes on her—a middle-aged woman wearing a black dress robe and a veil over her face. She never revealed her name. I always called her the Mistress of Darkness, since she had appeared from darkness. All she ever said to me when I was young was, "The more you keep thinking about it, the more I appear."

I didn't have a clue what she meant.

Then she would walk towards me, sit on the side of my bed, and put her hand on my cheek. "Such a pretty face," she would say, before vanishing into thin air, leaving me confused and worried.

I often had the same dream every single night. It was almost like this woman had to be there with me. I told Toby, and he thought she might be an old relative. I rejected his idea; there was no way this woman was related to me. But there was something about me she could sense. This kind of worried me, since she always gave me a creepy vibe every time she said, "Such a pretty face."

Toby said I should tell George and Nicole about this. A part of me wanted to, but another part of me wanted to run away from this chaos, in case I put George and Nicole in danger. I mean, the Mistress of Darkness didn't seem like much, but looks could be deceiving. And I loved George and Nicole dearly (even if they weren't my real parents). I would not allow them to put themselves in any kind of danger because of me.

Entering my teens, I became a bit more rebellious. The nightmares of the darkness still haunted me. So whenever I couldn't sleep, I'd write down my nightmares in the journal George and Nicole had gotten me for my birthday. I wrote about what I thought the darkness was and what it showed me. Most importantly, I wrote about the woman in black—the Mistress of Darkness—who, at the end of the dream, always placed her hand on my cheek and said, "Such a pretty face." Her words always left me confused. Why would she say this, especially about me?

George and Nicole Find the Journal

One beautiful Saturday morning, Scarlet went out to hang around with some friends from school. As George was about to leave for his office, something in her room caught his eye. It was her journal. Its pages explained her fear of the darkness, her nightmares, and the woman in black.

George's eyes were glued to the pages. When Nicole came upstairs carrying a tray with a sandwich and a cup of coffee for George, she noticed him looking at something and gently asked, "George, is everything okay, honey?"

George turned around and showed her Scarlet's journal.

Nicole set aside the tray and read the entire journal. She couldn't help but let loose a few tears. She was both sad and shocked. All that Scarlet had written seemed convincingly true, since Scarlet wasn't one to lie. Nicole turned back to her husband, who was at a loss for words. He held his arms out and embraced his wife gently as tears flowed down her face.

"What do we do?" she asked.

George knew what he was thinking would upset Scarlet, but this was serious. If he really loved her as his daughter, he'd want her to be safe. "I'll take this journal to the medic at work. Maybe he can figure out what's going on with her," he replied softly. He knew he would feel nothing but regret when Scarlet found out what he had done.

She Feels the Darkness Watching

At the age of seventeen, I could leave the house and have a bit of a social life, rather than hide from the darkness in the house. While hanging out with my friends one afternoon, I felt uneasy. I wasn't sure if it was the smell of alcohol and the smoke from the cigarettes making me feel nauseated and suffocated or if it was something else. I sat on the couch, trying to relax my head and have a good time.

My close friend Tiffany Pattington walked towards me and sat next to me. She handed me a glass of vodka and Coke. "Are you all right?" she asked.

I smiled and nodded as we clinked our glasses.

I began taking sips from my glass, and there she was—the woman from my nightmares. I kept telling myself I was hallucinating; she wasn't actually there. I slowly began to walk backwards, not taking my eyes off her as she smiled at me.

Not paying attention to where I was going, I ended up bumping into the class president and most popular boy Chase Davis. From the looks of him, he was as drunk as a homeless man on Christmas Eve.

I cringed at his drunkenness as he stumbled towards me, putting his arm around me. "Ha ha. Hey, beautiful, you should really watch where you're going." He laughed, and some group he was with all started laughing out their arses.

With him distracted, I diverted my attention. I needed to look behind me to see if that woman was still there. I took a deep breath and glanced in the direction where she had been standing.

She was gone. I wasn't going mad, was I? *I couldn't be*, I told myself. *But why is this happening to me?*

I needed some air. I started to walk away from the class president and his posse, but he grabbed me by the arm.

Tiffany saw him and walked over. When she gave him a good hard slap right across his face, everyone looked shocked. Ignoring them, she extended her hand towards me. I had dropped into a chair, taken aback and a little shocked by all that had happened. I grabbed her hand, and she helped me up.

"Come on, Scarlet. I'll give you a ride home," she said.

I followed her out of the building to her pink mini.

As I was about to get into the passenger's side, there she was again. Only this time she was in front of the car just staring at me, like she was waiting for me. I quickly got in the car, and Tiffany drove off, leaving the woman in black to simply watch from the distance until she dissolved into the darkness.

How Could They?

When I made it back home, it occurred to me that I now knew the Mistress of Darkness was watching my every move. I was more nervous than ever. At least I could write everything about the darkness. And maybe I could be stronger—strong enough that it wouldn't be able to sense my fears and nightmares.

I went to open the door with my key, but it was already unlocked. I quietly opened the door and reached for the light switch. When the light made everything visible, I saw George and Nicole, George holding my written pages in his hands, along with two strangers, one of them wearing a white jacket. I was devastated. They had finally found out what I had been writing about the darkness and about my nightmares.

The stranger in the white jacket stepped towards me. He could tell by looking into my eyes the things I'd been through. "It's all right," he said, adding, "We can help you, young lady."

The only emotion this sentence produced in me was anger. Upset, I marched towards George and Nicole, the tears building up in my eyes "Why? Why would you do this?" I asked, demanding that they answer me.

Nicole gave me a very apologetic look. Then she tried to wrap her arms around me. I pushed her away, my anger filling my veins. I felt more and more upset. It seemed I was always thinking, *Why?*

Along with attempting to get answers from them, I told them that everything I had written was true. I also told them about what I had seen at the party. All the doctor could say was that I was suffering from hallucinations from the insomnia I had developed.

Two Different Explanations

The medic, Dr Liam Holland, didn't agree with what the doctor had suggested. He thought this young lady seemed strong enough to control her emotions, which seemed to be making this darkness stronger. The doctor seemed to think it was nothing but a joke. The medic thought differently. He'd had many years of experience with mental trauma and insomnia as the cause of hallucinations.

After a private chat with George and Nicole, Dr Holland concluded that Scarlet's nightmares and trauma had led to her insomnia problem and that her case was worth looking into. He also thought he could teach Scarlet how to control her emotions and discipline her mind. That way, she could stop feeling so weak when it came to the darkness. In addition, they might learn more about what she saw in the darkness and try to study it.

Holland Protects

Dr Holland felt insulted by what Dr Colvin had said about this girl's problem. No matter how ridiculous Dr Colvin thought the apparition sounded, this girl needed help. He, it seemed, was the only one willing to offer that help. He didn't know what feeling he had for this girl, but she reminded him of his daughter, who he had lost a couple of years ago.

George and Nicole were convinced that Scarlet needed help. And if Dr Holland had the right idea, which George believed he did, she would have to go with him. It didn't take long for them to make a decision. She had to go. But at least she would be in good hands, and she'd be loved. That was all Nicole wanted.

She understood that Scarlet would have no idea how to properly react, and she feared that, when they told her she had to leave, she would feel betrayed.

Scarlet cried when they told her. All Nicole wanted to do when she saw Scarlet in tears was to hold her in her arms. But she knew that, if she did, Scarlet would push her away again. There was nothing either she or George could do. They wanted to follow Dr Holland's plan for helping Scarlet. And it was him who promised her face-to-face that she would be protected and, most importantly, safe.

"Nobody can protect me." It was all I could say. I couldn't believe what I was hearing. I felt so betrayed. Anger filled my veins, and tears streamed down my cheeks.

Looking around, I could see that everybody in the room was shocked at what I had said.

Then Dr Holland knelt down beside where I was sitting on the couch and took my hands and promised I would be safe.

I was taken aback when I stared into Dr Holland's hazel eyes, which had a hint of blue. They say the eyes are the windows to the soul for a reason. What I saw in his eyes was kindness, compassion, and determination—everything that described Nathaniel. If only my big brother was still alive. And then there was what the Mistress of Darkness believed, which I still feared—that through the darkness she'd bring back Nathaniel.

I was about to speak up. But my head started to throb as images of the day Nathaniel died rushed into my mind. The Mistress of Darkness stood beside him. He tried to get away from her. Then she smiled at me, and all I could hear was the echoes of her voice saying, "Such a pretty face."

Scarlet's first session

When I'd started feeling woozy and the room had started to go dark, Dr Holland and George had carried me to his car. Nicole had burst into tears. Her oldest son, Conner, had held her in his arms. Just before I'd blacked out completely, I'd caught a glimpse of her eyes and had seen her disbelief—as if she was thinking that, no matter how much love she had given to protect me, it wasn't enough; it was never enough.

I wasn't sure how much time had past since then. But now I was lying on a bed in a very plain room. Out of the corner of my eye, I saw that there were security cameras in each corner of the room. *Someone must be watching me*, I thought. I carefully walked around the room. There was a desk with a computer on it. And on the desk was my journal—the journal containing all I had written about my nightmares and the Mistress of Darkness.

While I was looking through my journal, Dr Holland, or Liam as he liked to be called, entered the room and sat on the chair next to me. "Is everything okay, young lady?" he asked.

I asked him about what had happened to me and how I had gotten here. Luckily, he was true to his word and told me everything that had happened.

He also mentioned that I had been muttering a lot, talking about Nathaniel as if I was trying to save him from the darkness. This, he said, was only goading my fears, making the darkness of the Mistress of

Darkness stronger. And stupid girl that I was, I couldn't help but be afraid, even though I was trying to be stronger. But the Mistress of Darkness knew how to get to me.

I tried to wipe away the tears, and Liam held me in his arms and comforted me. I started to feel better as I hugged him back.

He glanced at his watch. "It's almost time for your first session," he said gently.

Getting up, he opened the door like a gentleman and let me go first.

"Session?" I asked, stepping out into the hallway tentatively.

"You'll see," he said and then led me to a room I would soon become familiar with.

Inside the room, Liam and two science-type techies sat me on a chair. Then they placed on my head a mysterious-looking headband that was connected to the computers in the other room.

Once I was hooked up, Liam reassured me one last time. I'm not gonna lie. I was scared. My mind was filled with questions. What was I about to see? Would they be able to see her as well? Then they'd know that everything I had written about my nightmares was true.

As soon as they switched on the machine, my head started to throb. Memories rushed through my mind, and darkness surrounded them like a predator stalking its prey. The only memory that wasn't surrounded by darkness was the same memory I'd been having nightmares about for years now. Liam and the others could see on their monitors what I was seeing.

Their minds were blown as they continued to monitor what was happening. Liam used the microphone to communicate to me from the other room. "I know it's frightening to you. But it's okay," he told me. "We're here."

He spoke reassuringly to me until the Mistress of Darkness faded from my mind and the monitors, moving seamlessly into the room I was in. She turned slowly to face Liam and the scientists.

───────◆◆»«◆◆───────

Liam couldn't help but let out a shocked gasp. Telling the two scientists to keep an eye on what was going on, he rushed toward the other room. He had to get Scarlet out of there.

───────◆◆»«◆◆───────

The Mistress of Darkness heard the banging on the door. She faced me and reached out to touch me on my cheek. I tried to resist, telling myself over and over that I wasn't afraid and that the mistress wasn't real. But that only seemed to anger her even more.

Finally, Liam burst through the door and unplugged the equipment. As soon as it was over, he took off the headband and wrapped his arms around me. Tears were still pouring down my face.

"It's okay, he said gently. "It's over. You're gonna be okay."

All I could say was, "How can it be over?"

Good News Too Late

The day after Scarlet went with Liam Holland, Nicole was filled with doubt about herself. She sat on the edge of Scarlet's bed, wondering whether sending her to Liam had been a good idea.

The more she thought about it, the more sorrow and guilt she felt. Tears slowly flowed down her face.

When it was time for the mail to arrive, Nicole went downstairs to check the post. She noticed a certain envelope that was addressed to both her and George. She opened the letter. As soon as she started to read it, tears filled her eyes. She fell to her knees, where she stayed until George came through the back door and saw his beloved wife on her knees in tears.

George walked towards Nicole and knelt down besides her. Wrapping his arms around her, he gently and calmly asked what was wrong.

After a few minutes, she managed to settle her emotions down. She handed the letter to George. This answered his question. He embraced his wife again, and they both pondered the good news that had come too late.

The letter was an adoption approval from the social services office and the orphanage where Scarlet had lived before she had come to them. It gave approval for George and Nicole to become the rightful parents of Scarlet Daphne Jayden.

That night, George and Nicole told Conner, Jodie, and Toby the news. The boys were pleased to have another sibling.

Jodie, though, felt a slight sensation of guilt; when Scarlet had first come to live with them, she hadn't exactly been thrilled. Now, she only wished that, one day, she'd see Scarlet again and make amends with her little sister.

Liam Studies Scarlet's Journal

After Scarlet's first session, Liam had asked her to borrow that journal of hers. At first, she had been wary, not sure she wanted him to even take a glance at it. It was clearly rather personal to her. On top of that, as Liam knew, it would take Scarlet awhile to trust him. Not only did she have the typical teenage stubbornness; she was also quite shy around strangers.

Liam took his time and started to get to know her a bit. Their interactions developed into something almost like a father-daughter relationship. This was touching for Liam, since he'd lost his daughter to cancer.

Liam opened up to Scarlet. When he told her about his daughter, she clearly felt sorrow for him. She had begun to open up and talk about the orphanage she and Nathaniel had been sent to.

Liam was curious about the type of life Scarlet and her brother had had before they'd gone to the orphanage. But she wouldn't say much, other than that Nathaniel had protected her from someone. This piqued Liam's curiosity quite a bit.

Liam continued to promise to help her though this trauma, hoping she would come to trust him.

One night, Scarlet came into his office and handed him her journal. At first, he was taken by surprise. As he held her journal in his hands, he said reassuringly, "I promise you, Scarlet, I will help you the best I can."

Liam read the journal all night, trying to understand what this darkness was and who the hell this Mistress of Darkness was.

As he read and reread the journal, he scoured the Internet, looking for some information matching what the darkness was.

He read myths, legends of paranormal entities, and old Christian tales about darkness. But the different forms of darkness mentioned on these sites had nothing on what Scarlet described.

So Liam worked hard, often working all night, trying to uncover anything he could that might relate to Scarlet's situation. He placed sticky notes inside the journal whenever he found a theory that seemed similar to Scarlet's descriptions. He nearly turned his desk upside down as he scanned through each description and every piece of information he could. Then he placed everything he'd found inside a strongbox for Scarlet.

Chapter 2

Friendship

Nathaniel Used

After several sessions, I was getting nowhere. Somehow, the darkness was always one step ahead. I tried to block it out, but it always found another way round to me.

Then Liam had an idea. He said I should try and communicate with Nathaniel through my dreams.

So I did. Every night was the same. I would cry out Nathaniel's name, begging him to answer, begging for something that would allow me to communicate with him.

One night, as soon as I stopped, he appeared right in front of me—at least I thought it was him for a moment.

When I saw dark smoke around his eyes, I instantly knew what had happened. The darkness knew about Nathaniel. And so it had possessed his body to get to me by messing with my emotions, saying to me that I could bring Nathaniel back, if I only did what the darkness told me to do.

I spent the last couple of days in my room, thinking about what the darkness wanted and what I'd have to do to bring Nathaniel back from the dead. My emotions were torn. My heart had started to ache, and my head began to throb. I knew that Nathaniel couldn't come back to life. I kept screaming that out at every nightmare. I had to prove a point to the darkness.

I was then confronted with the Mistress of Darkness, this time wearing different attire. Although she still wore a veil on her face, the dark robes she always appeared in were replaced by a long black ballgown. I tried not to pay attention. Then her eyes began to glow a blood-red colour. She knelt down next to me and ever so slowly extended her hand to touch my cheek again. I quickly slapped her hand away.

During the sessions I'd been having, Liam had taught me to stand up for myself against my fear of the darkness. And it was working. I was able to resist the temptation of the darkness, even though it kept on fighting, using my own memories against me. I still fought. I wasn't gonna let this fear drive me to insanity.

This time, all I could do was run. The darkness crept quickly behind me. Suddenly, I found myself on a ledge. I couldn't see anything but darkness. When I turned back, Nathaniel appeared in front of me again. But there was something different. He was no longer a child. He now looked like a full-grown man in his twenties.

Even more disturbing, he still had his childlike voice, which echoed every time he spoke. The Mistress of Darkness stood next to him. I no longer felt afraid. Somehow, my fear had turned to anger. I wanted to lunge at her. But I couldn't. The darkness was beginning to manipulate my mind. I didn't want to take orders from it. So I fell from the ledge and woke up from the nightmare I was in.

Liam and the General

Scarlet had written down everything that had happened to her. At first Liam couldn't believe what he was reading. But he did after those sessions and after he had seen the Mistress of Darkness himself. He was proud of Scarlet for being brave.

But he knew she had to be much stronger to fight this fear. The fact that the darkness was manipulating her mind made him feel sick to his stomach. He couldn't let this happen to such a sweet girl like Scarlet. He couldn't let her be this way. She needed all the help she could get. It was time to speak to the general.

General Howard was not a man you could easily please. He was a right hard-ass. But Liam knew that he was a good man inside, no matter what some of the others said. He was good at his job. The soldiers at his command followed him well, and he led them well.

Liam walked boldly into General Howard's office, demanding that he let Scarlet into his ranks. He spoke of her potential and what she was suffering through.

General Howard's eyes widened as Liam Holland talked about his patient. He remembered that some of his veteran soldiers had the same type of problem. He'd seen with his own eyes those soldiers being so manipulated that it drove them to insanity. In some terrible cases, he'd had no choice but to have them committed—for their own safety and for that of the new recruits.

After Liam left his office, General Howard pondered for a bit. From what he'd heard, this young lady had potential. But the manipulating fear of the darkness was a concern. This was a difficult case.

Still, after reading Liam's reports on the sessions, General Howard saw that Scarlet definitely needed help. And he was willing to let her into his ranks.

Having made his decision, he reached for his phone. He searched his contacts for Liam's number. As soon as the phone rang, Liam answered.

"Bring her to my office tomorrow morning," General Howard said.

"Yes, sir," Liam replied.

Scarlet Meets the General

As I walked with Liam through the army boot camp, I was being stared at constantly. This made me feel like I was not welcome here. When I told Liam I felt uncomfortable, he just put his arm around me and said, "Ignore them."

Liam was truly a kind-hearted gentleman and a brilliant father figure to me. In some ways, he was more like a father to me than George Fenderson. He even loved me like I was his daughter. After all, he had been a father once. His original daughter had passed away. An aggressive form of cancer had taken her away from him and his wife.

Soon, we had made it to General Howard's office. It was clear that, as soon as he laid eyes on me, he saw the potential and passion I had. Plus, I told him about my problem, adding in some details that Liam had left out.

General Howard gestured for Liam to leave the room. When he was gone, General Howard put his arm around me and flicked a switch on his desk. A hidden passage opened behind his bookcase. Looking through it, I saw a completely different place.

It gave off a very modern laboratory / secret organisation feel, which, to be honest, made me a bit uncomfortable at first. At the same time, though, I was completely amazed.

Seeing how shocked I was as I first laid eyes on this strange place, General Howard let out a slight chuckle. "It's quite a sight," he said.

I questioned him about this place and why it had been built. He explained as we walked around that it was the headquarters of an organisation that combined the army, the CIA, and the FBI. This organisation, the Central Forensic Agency, or simply the CFA, enabled those agencies to work together to take down corporate scumbag terrorist warlords.

We then entered a section known as the paranormal department, where behind glass walls in one of the rooms scientists were doing tests on traumatised and demented civilians and soldiers, who were screaming out crazy shit. The scientists were trying to cure these subjects' supernatural traumas, General Howard told me. I was taken aback by what I was hearing and seeing.

Suddenly, I started to feel like I was being tricked. I turned to the general and burst out angrily, "Whatever Liam's told you about me, I'm nothing like them." As I said this, I pointed towards the demented patients and looked forcefully into General Howard's eyes.

"Mr Holland's told me small details," the general snapped. "Now don't you ever speak to me in that tone, young lady." He was clearly offended by my words.

Sure General Howard seemed like a nice guy. But looks could be deceiving. At first, I was thrown by his angry outburst at my perceived accusation. I may have been a sweet and innocent girl still, but I was almost eighteen-year-old girl now, and I wasn't having any of it. I could tell by General Howard's words what he had in mind. He was thinking that, if I ever became unstable, he'd have me put in a padded cell.

I was upset—no not upset; I was furious. Tears flowed down my face. Looking at that supernatural trauma department room, I wondered, What if I couldn't trust any of these people and they thought I was nothing but a lunatic with a childish imagination?

———◆◆◆———

Though he also felt a hint of sorrow, General Howard felt incredibly angry. If it wasn't for his close friend Neil, who was working in one of the labs, the general would have thrown a punch.

Anger

From outside the general's office, Liam heard the commotion. He threw open the door and followed the noise into an entirely new room. When he spotted Scarlet, sobbing and looking frightened, he was furious.

He closed in on the general, clenched his fist, and punched him to the ground. As the captain got to his feet, Liam looked at the surrounding area, taking in the supernatural department.

"What were you thinking?" Liam shouted. "She's going through enough. Now you wanna get her committed? You son of a—"

Liam threw another punch, but General Howard deflected it. Grabbing Liam's arm, he quickly lowered it and pushed him away. Then he dusted himself off and explained to Liam what was going on.

Nevertheless, Liam wasn't buying it. He saw what kind of man General Howard was. If there were a slight problem involving Scarlet and the darkness, he'd have her locked up and tested on.

Scarlet Touched

Liam had apparently had enough of the general's explanations. He took me to meet the squad I'd be teaming up with and training with. First, there was twenty-seven-year-old Kirsten Roland. An expert marine sniper, she had 113 confirmed kills in Iraq and Afghanistan. The guy cleaning his glasses was a twenty-five-year-old ex-FBI forensics researcher turned fully qualified CIA tech field agent. His name was Matthew Tyran. Last but not least was a thirty-four-year-old drill instructor who was also a navy veteran named Harry Armanton.

After I introduced myself to the team, I excused myself and headed into the bathrooms. At the sinks, I splashed handfuls of water over my face as I cried out all the anger that had built up inside me over the interaction with the general.

Then suddenly I heard her voice in my head. "Join me pretty girl," she said sinisterly.

"Get out of my head!" I screamed in anger.

I then saw her in the mirror. She wore a mysterious smirk on her face. Then suddenly, she seemed to extend her hand from the mirror. As always, I refused to accept her touch. She became more and more frustrated. "You will join me," she growled.

She kept on at me, saying I could get what I wanted if I joined her. But I refused to surrender to her.

She grew angrier and angrier, twisting my emotions as she tried to persuade me.

"I will never join you"—I took a deep breath as I stared deeply into her eyes—"you monster."

The Mistress of Darkness was beginning to lose her patience, as I kept refusing her offer. Then Nathaniel appeared right in front of me. I quickly moved away, screaming at the hallucination of Nathaniel. "No! You're not you! You're dead. Do you hear? You're *dead*!"

I felt like I was losing my mind—that the Mistress of Darkness was trying everything to get me to surrender to her.

I still tried to block her out of my head, but the voices were getting louder and louder. My head began to throb, and it was beginning to make me feel sick. My body felt weak. I lay on the floor holding my head, trying not to listen to the voices or see the visions she was making me have.

Liam was getting worried. He rushed to the bathroom where Scarlet was. What he heard made his eyes widen. He tried to burst open the door. When he couldn't get in, he called over Kirsten, Matthew, and Harry to help. But the door was jammed tight; the darkness was obviously blocking it to keep people out while it was manipulating Scarlet.

Kirsten, Matthew, and Harry hadn't seen anything like this before and were wondering to themselves what this darkness was all about. Why was it after Scarlet? And more importantly, what did it want with her?

<hr>

The possessed hallucination of Nathaniel kept talking to me, saying, "Please, little sis, save me. I'm not really dead; you need to save me. I thought you loved me, little sis." Nathaniel's voice echoed in my mind. All I kept saying was that nothing was real. Nathaniel wasn't real. My final words were as clear as day, which made the mistress flare up in anger. As my eyes widened, I cried, "The Mistress of Darkness isn't real."

After I said that, she became angry and appeared right in front of me next to Nathaniel. As she walked towards me, I tried to back away, until I found myself trapped in a corner. She knelt down, extended her hands, and placed them on my cheeks. Bringing her head down to me, she gently left a kiss on my forehead. Then she smirked; she finally had me in the palm of her hand. I was now the darkness's puppet. I was now under her control.

As I lay down on the bathroom floor, even though my eyesight was blurred, I could tell she was smiling at me. She took my hand and gently whispered, "I'll be coming for you for your trials."

I was completely dazed. It felt like I was hypnotised as I slowly nodded in response.

She smiled again and knelt down again. "That's a good girl," she said, tapping my shoulder.

Then all of a sudden, she vanished into thin air. I lay on the freezing cold floor, my eyes slightly closed. I could barely see.

I felt drained of all my energy. Every muscle in my body ached. I felt like I had done twenty hours of exercise. My joints felt stiff and burned, and lying on the cold floor made them burn even more. I was in agony.

I vaguely heard Liam and the others finally break through the bathroom door. There was commotion as Liam rushed towards me, and I heard him shout to one of the others to get a doctor.

Scarlet to Medical

Kirsten and Matt froze in place when they saw Scarlet lying there in front of them. They couldn't imagine how terrible this darkness must be.

Harry wasted no time and rushed off to get medical help. As terrible as it sounded, he couldn't bear to look at Scarlet in her horrific state.

Liam carefully picked her up. Holding her in his arms, he followed Harry to the medical quarters.

I was beginning to wake up. I would soon learn that it had been a couple of hours since the incident in the bathroom. At first, my reaction was pure shock. I wanted to get up and see where I was. But I was gently pushed back down by a woman, who said gently, "Whoa. Take it easy, Miss Jayden."

My vision was blurry, and the idea of Nathaniel still alive and trapped by the Mistress of Darkness still echoed in my mind. "What …? Who are you?" I sounded delirious.

"I've just given you a sedative. Please, Miss Jayden, you must remain calm. Dr Holland said you had another episode. But don't worry. You're safe now."

That's all I heard her say, as I fell back into unconsciousness.

A couple of hours had past again, and I finally fully regained consciousness. When I woke up, Kirsten, Matthew, and Harry were beside the bed I was on. I still felt a little fuzzy, and my mind was in a blur. When they asked me what had happened, I couldn't exactly answer. My mind felt like it was burning, like it was being torn from a massive hangover.

"Listen," I managed to say, "I know you're worried and want to know what happened to me. But I can't fully remember."

I was able to stand, but my legs felt like jelly. I nearly fell to my knees, but Kirsten and Harry caught me and stood me up straight. As I regained my posture, Kirsten smiled at me. "Take it easy, Scarlet," she said reassuringly. She reminded me of my high school best friend, Tiffany, but she seem to have more of an attitude than Tiffany.

As for Harry, he didn't seem right. There was something off about the way he watched me.

Harry stepped back after having helped Scarlet get her balance. Watching Scarlet's traumatic episode had somehow made him feel wrong.

But he brushed it aside, pretending that everything was fine. After all, Scarlet needed all the support she could get.

Still, he couldn't stand the thought of being near her if something like that massive psychotic episode she'd had were to happen again.

General Howard Gets Suspicious

General Howard had heard what happened to Scarlet Jayden. He was becoming more and more suspicious. Ever since her episode, he had avoided speaking to her entirely, giving her no more than a slight glimpse.

From what he had seen while she was training, he was impressed with her determination. But that didn't matter. She couldn't be trusted. Although he had mentioned to her that some of his veterans suffered something slightly similar, it wasn't the same to him. At least their struggles were a result of war and loss.

General Howard went back into his office and opened up his left side drawer. He picked up his hip flask, which was filled with his favourite brand of whiskey. Whenever he ever felt angry or, in this case, suspicious, he'd take a sip from his hip flask.

As I continued my training, there were moments where I would start to pass out. General Howard had the nerve to ignore my problem, but that was okay. My guardian angel, Dr Liam Holland, was always watching from the sidelines, not to mention that the squad I was with was always looking out for me.

———◆◆◆◆———

Harry was torn. He wanted Scarlet to do her best. But another side of him wanted to ask General Howard to dismiss her from the squad. The thought made him feel wrong, though.

———◆◆◆◆———

Two months had rolled by since Scarlet first came to the army barracks, and General Howard still didn't trust her. He pretended to be nice. But inside, his gut was telling him she was trouble. Her mental disorder made her even more suspicious in his eyes.

As for her squad mates, Mr Tyran and Ms Roland were two very valuable assets to the CFA. First, there was Ms Roland. General Howard had known she'd probably latch onto Miss Jayden, given her sexuality and the likeliness that there'd be an attraction there. But Howard admired her; she was, after all, the CFA's best US Marine sniper, with 113 confirmed kills. He realised, too, that he could never antagonise her.

As for Mr Tyran, that young man could hack his way into an enemy base and shut down every security system without the enemy knowing. There were some good hackers in the CFA, but Mr Tyran was the best the CFA had.

General Howard was just about to take another pull from his hip flask, when he paused and watched Scarlet from his window. "I'll be keeping my eye on you, Miss Jayden," he said, sounding rather crude.

Good Friends Make Good Allies

It had been a couple months since I'd had that psychotic episode on my first day here. I was in my room studying for a test I had tomorrow morning. On top of that, I had my final practical test in the afternoon. I was about to start my early morning routine—push-ups at 6 a.m., followed by a morning jog around the apartment blocks.

Ever since that horrible experience, my mind would periodically become a little fuzzy, and I kept getting flashbacks. I tried to sort through them and remember what had happened. But all I kept thinking was that Nathaniel was still alive and that I had a chance to save him.

My heart and mind were torturing me with my emotions. It felt like I was being torn apart. I didn't know what to do. I mean, of course Nathaniel was my brother, and I loved him. Another side of me knew there was something wrong about this idea that was stuck in my head. But it was always there, in the back of my head.

Even if I successfully ignored it one day, it would end up coming back the next day. I told Kirsten and Matthew about what had happened, since they demanded to know; they had never seen anything like this before. Harry was not really interested. He had been more and more distant with me. I would come to find out that he was even thinking of moving to another squad—until Liam confronted him.

<hr />

"What on earth do you think you're doing?"

Harry frowned. He was insulted by Liam's words. Pushing him away, he snapped, "What does it look I'm doing? I'm moving to a different squad."

Liam couldn't believe Harry was even considering this. Harry was a good and loyal man; now he was being more selfish than loyal.

Aware of what Liam was probably thinking, Harry softened his tone. "If that girl goes down," he said with a sigh, "I do not want to be the one doing colour combination when she finally hits the floor."

Liam explained to Harry that Scarlet needed all the support she could get. Maybe that could help her against the fear of this darkness.

But Harry was having none of it. He couldn't stop recalling images of his closest friend back when he'd served in the navy—images of the trauma his friend had endured. The memories terrified Harry, reminding him that his friend had been so lost in trauma he had become a stranger to his own best friend. He shook his head.

"She needs help," Liam urged, explaining in detail the darkness confronting Scarlet and the Mistress of Darkness, which was what Scarlet always called the apparition that haunted her. He insisted that help and support was imperative.

Still, Harry wasn't sure. He needed more time to think about whether to remain with the squad or move on.

Chapter 3

Hallucinations

Scarlet Attacked in Her Sleep

I still felt drowsy. I'd spent most of the night reviewing for my test. Plus I could barely get a wink of sleep ever since that episode in the bathroom. The insomnia had become nearly unbearable; some nights, I hardly got any sleep at all.

Whenever I did fall asleep, I would usually find myself in a house or in a field in pitch-black darkness. And she was always there as well. I would look around, searching for a way out until I would stumble upon a torch.

In fact, there it was now. As I held the flashlight in my hand, I caught a glimpse of her. She looked angry. Lifting her arms above her head, she clapped her hands together. Behind her, a gust of darkness had gathered like a tornado. She extended her arms in my direction, and the tornado of darkness gusted towards me like a hurricane approaching a shoreline.

I held the flashlight in my hands like a lightsaber from *Star Wars*. As soon as I flicked the switch on the flashlight, the light beamed towards the gust of darkness. It felt the cold in the bright light. It screeched like it was in agonising pain.

The flashlight felt heavy in my hands as I shined its light into the darkness. I started to feel dizzy and light-headed. I was about to fall to my knees. Then I saw that Nathaniel was standing in front of me with his hand extended to me. I considered taking his hand, but I didn't. The darkness was using him again. It would never stop toying with my emotions.

The Mistress of Darkness whispered in my ear, "It's time pretty girl."

I quickly got away from her by hitting her on the head with the flashlight. She glared daggers at me. I turned my head in all directions, trying to find an escape route.

Suddenly I heard a familiar voice. I tried to process what I was hearing. Who was calling my name? The voice became clearer. It was Kirsten who was calling me. Without any hesitation, I bolted past the mistress and Nathaniel.

The look on the woman's face was one of pure rage. She commanded the gust of darkness to come after me. I continued to run towards Kirsten's voice. As soon as I reached the bright light, Kirsten's voice echoing in my ears, the gust of darkness caused the light to flickered out. I could still hear Kirsten's voice, though, and I wasn't gonna let the Mistress of Darkness stop me from waking up from this nightmare.

"You'll never stop me," I cried. "Someday I'll end you—for good." I continued to run towards the next spot of light I could see. As I extended my hand towards it, I suddenly awoke, gasping for breath.

Friends Stick Together

Kirsten was there, her hands on my shoulders. "Easy, Scarlet," she said. "It's okay. You had another nightmare."

I looked at her, and she looked at me.

"It felt like more than a nightmare," I replied, still gasping as I rubbed my eyes. Looking around, I saw that I had dozed off at my desk. This was the fourth time this week. *Thank you, Mistress of Darkness, you old hag*, I thought sarcastically.

Kirsten was a good friend, and she kind of reminded me of Tiffany. They shared similar traits. Both of them were honest and kind, not to mention a bit stubborn. But Kirsten just seemed a bit too bold. She was the kind of person who would brag to all the men how great she was. Typical Kirsten.

Even though I had been sleeping, I felt like I had been awake all night. When I went to stand up, I collapsed to my knees. My head was throbbing in agony. I had another flash of imagery. But this time, I saw the well that

Nathaniel had fallen down. This was followed by a vision of the Mistress of Darkness extending her hand towards me.

There was one thing that didn't make sense. That day when she was manipulating me in the bathroom, the darkness had touched me. My mind hadn't been able to process properly since that day. But if she really had touched me, did that mean that she was able to switch me into zombie mode with the snap of her fingers?

———◆▸❈◂◆———

I composed myself and got dressed for my usual morning ritual. After I finished my jog, I took a shower and met Kirsten in the mess hall for breakfast. I grabbed myself a cup of coffee and sat down next to Kirsten, who was, understandably, full of questions.

Soon, Matthew came along and joined us at the table. "You girls okay?" He smiled politely at me.

Kirsten glanced between me and Matthew and let out a slight giggle.

I tried not to notice. "We're fine, aren't we, Kirsten?" I casually smiled.

Kirsten glanced at Matt and me, still giggling. Then she composed herself and responded to my reply with a nod.

I saw Matthew glance at her. He seemed to have an idea what she was giggling about, which made him blush a bit.

After that, Kirsten had an idea. She suggested that she and I go for a girls' night out. I pondered that for a minute. The last time I had gone for a night out, I had continually hallucinated about the Mistress of Darkness. I considered what the mistress might do if I did go on this girls' night out with Kirsten.

"I don't think that's a good idea," I exclaimed.

Kirsten and Matthew looked at me with confused expressions, as if they were demanding an explanation.

So I told them. I didn't want to tell them, but they were the only people I could trust. And it wasn't like I had any other options.

After I'd told them about the last time I had gone out, Matthew got up from his seat. Sitting next to me, he put his arm around my shoulder. "I can't imagine the things you're going through," he said. "But there's one thing I can say. You're not alone. We're here for you, Scarlet. Whoever this Mistress of Darkness is, she'll never break us apart, as long as we stick together."

Kirsten put her arm around my shoulder too. "Matthew's right," she said. "No matter what happens, we'll always be here for each other."

"Oh my God. Are you high?" Matthew joked. "'Cause you're getting mushy," he added. Kirsten was typically a tough broad, and her display of affection seemed to amuse him.

Kirsten leaned over and punched Matthew on the arm.

We both giggled at his reaction, and then we all laughed together.

No Such Thing as Celebration

This morning at the mess hall table had been the first time I had laughed like that in a while. Kirsten and Matthew really did care about me.

I wasn't sure about Harry. He had become distant. Sure, he'd been there during training and had helped me prepare for the practical test, which I was about to take. But he had no choice. He was my drill instructor, after all.

I would later learn that he was still struggling. Being confronted by Liam had made him questions himself. He knew he wasn't being the loyal good-hearted man he normally was. Rather, he saw in the mirror a selfish man. The thought of being so selfish made him shiver, as if he was a victim in some crazy horror story.

I had passed the theory part of the test that morning, and I was doing last-minute preparations for my practical exam. I felt someone place a hand on my shoulder. "Good luck, Scarlet."

I looked up, and to my surprise, there was Harry, smiling at me. It was a reassuring smile. I realised it was the first time he had actually smiled at me. At first, I was a bit confused.

Ever since I'd had that horrible manipulation episode, Harry seemed to keep his distance. It wasn't like that at all with Matthew and Kirsten, who were very supportive. Harry just seemed blinded by something. Matthew had once told me that Harry had lost one of his best friends due to a serious traumatic experience during his time in the navy, not to mention that he was a veteran. So there was no doubt that he had witnessed other traumatic experiences.

No time to think about that now. I had a test to take.

I got through it with ease, all thanks to my training.

General Howard congratulated me and promoted me to private—Private Scarlet Jayden. But as soon as he had done so, he left the arena.

That was when the middle-aged crone began to whisper in my ear. Her words were icy and dark. They rang in my ears. I felt the colour drain from my face. My legs felt like jelly, and my vision became blurry. I fell to my knees.

—◆◆✕◆●—

Harry watched in sheer dread and horror as Scarlet dropped to the ground in the middle of the arena. He couldn't bear being anywhere near her when she was like this.

Matthew, who had also noticed her fall, bolted past Harry, heading towards the centre of the arena. "What the hell is wrong with you?" he called.

Despite the disappointment in Matthew's voice, Harry backed away. He was simultaneously horrified and insulted by Matthew's words.

Matthew knelt down next to Scarlet. Harry could see from a distance that he was talking to her as he wrapped his arm around her and placed his hand on her shoulder. When she remained unresponsive, Matthew picked her up and ran towards the medical quarters.

In a Dark Place

I had no idea where I was. I wasn't on the dark field or in the dark abandoned house. All I could hear was her icy voice echoing in my ears. Then suddenly, she caught me off guard and grabbed me by the neck. The moment she touched me, I felt a cloud of darkness flow around me, keeping me contained within it.

She extended her hand and touched my cheek. I tried to resist, but her flowing cloud of darkness prevented me from resisting.

"I'm very disappointed in you, young lady." I could hear the frustration in her voice.

I tried not to listen. "Go to hell. I'm not talking," I responded angrily. And I spat in her face.

"I don't want to fight you. But no matter. All those nights you were a frightful child, you've made me stronger." She leaned in closer to my ear and whispered, "Just wait until I call upon you for your trials. Nathaniel will be so pleased."

She then released me and began to walk away into the pitch-black darkness.

"Don't you dare hurt my brother," I shrieked. "Do you hear me? Do you hear me?! Come back here."

Despite all my shouting, all she did was turn and give me a devilish smirk before vanishing into the darkness.

I was all alone in this dark place. I collapsed to my hands and knees, crying out with all my anger. All I could feel was anger; I angry not only with the Mistress of Darkness, but I was also angry with myself. In particular, I was angry with my younger self for being so weak. Well that part wasn't so much anger as it was regret. I had been so unreliable and weak. Now look where it had gotten me.

Since then, the Mistress of Darkness had gotten stronger by feeding on my emotions. Ever since the day Nathaniel had passed, my life has been dipped in shit. I even thought about ending my own life as I cried out for her to just leave me alone.

Stay in the Light

Liam heard about Scarlet's collapse and rushed to the medical quarters. When he got there, he found Matthew sitting on a chair next to the bed Scarlet was in. Matthew looked worried as he watched Scarlet, who was unconscious, toss and turn and mumble.

Liam walked towards Scarlet. He knew what to do. He started talking to her, telling her to follow his voice and to come back to him.

———◆◆◆———

Meanwhile, in the dark place, a bright light shined behind me. I could hear Liam's voice coming from the light. As soon as I turned towards it, the Mistress of Darkness sent her hurricane of darkness after me. Glancing over my shoulder, I saw that it was getting closer. But I refused to let her stop me.

As soon as I reached for the light, I woke up. I sat up straight and gasped for breath. Liam had his arm around me, and his hand was on my shoulder. He gently pushed me back down. "It's okay, Scarlet. It's okay. You're safe," he reassured me.

But since I was still freaking out, Liam had no choice but to give me another sedative.

"I'm sorry, Scarlet," he said gently as I drifted back into unconsciousness.

———————◆◆)◆(◆◆———————

I found myself somewhere else. There was a bright light shining down on me. But everything outside the light was dark. All around me was nothing but pitch-black darkness. I glanced behind me, and I instantly recognised the building I could make out, just on the edge of the light. It was the children's home Nathaniel and I had been sent to.

It wasn't until *she* came out of the shadows that I realised how lucky I was to have this beam of light. Whenever she came too close, the light seemed to scorch her pale white skin, and the shadows around her screeched in agonising pain.

She grew frustrated that the light was protecting me. I'm not gonna lie. I couldn't help but gloat. Here I was bathed in the cold light around me, and there was no way she could come near me.

Growing more and more frustrated, she ordered her hurricane gust of darkness towards me. And as it made its way towards me, the light that was protecting me flickered out.

I had no choice but to run—with the hurricane gust of darkness fast on my heels.

I seemed to be able to make out faint patches of light here and there ahead of me in the darkness. But as I tried to focus on them, they kept going out.

Finally, I stumbled upon a flare gun, which I was pleased to see was already loaded with one flare. I pointed it at the hurricane-filled darkness and pulled the trigger. The flare exploded. The darkness screeched in horrific pain. Only then did I begin to regain consciousness as the light from the flare became brighter and brighter.

Liam's Farewell

Just before Scarlet was due to wake up from the sedative, Liam received a message that he was to see General Howard. When the general told him he was being sent to investigate a hidden village of Rharib Ail's Scasura in Afghanistan, Liam recalled his first tour to Afghanistan. Veterans had often talked about the place, and it was generally believed that some shady shite was going on there. There were stories of new recruits who went on patrol around the area and went missing.

Liam had to process what he was being asked to do. Going into that hidden village would most likely be a suicide mission; he figured he had a 99.9 percent chance of not making it back alive. He tried not to think too much about that.

Later on that night, he saw that Kirsten and Matthew were going back to the barracks. They looked at him with confused expressions until he gestured them over to him.

They had no choice but to follow him, though he was acting a bit strange.

Liam could see how surprised they were when he told them to look after Scarlet for him. He explained what they should do if she ever had another episode.

He was grateful that they agreed. Kirsten promised to fill Harry in on the details, though Liam had already given him an overview.

Before Matthew walked off, Liam called him once again. When Matthew stopped and came back, Liam asked him to follow him to his office, where he kept the strongbox that contained all his discoveries of the darkness. At first, Matthew was curious why he was there. When he started to ask what was going on, Liam simply ushered him into his office. He went immediately to his desk, opened his drawer, and gently took out the strongbox. He placed it in Matthew's hands.

"When Scarlet's ready, will you give her this?" Liam said.

All Matthew could do was nod. He tried to ask what was in it.

But Liam simply said, "That's only for Scarlet to know."

Matthew agreed to Liam's request, determined to keep his word. He placed the strongbox in his personal locker, ready for when Scarlet was ready—though he didn't feel quite right about it. It didn't seem fair for Scarlet to wait.

Even though he had a slight crush on Scarlet, he didn't want to lose their friendship. He didn't want it to be like his previous relationships from his high school and university years.

<hr/>

The next morning, Liam packed his essentials in his rucksack, put on his combat medic chest piece, hurled his rucksack over his shoulder, and exited his quarters.

While making his way to the Chinook helicopters, he bumped into Scarlet.

<hr/>

Liam was clearly lost in thought, as he literally walked into me. When he looked up and saw that it was me, he seemed shocked.

"I know," I said before he could say anything.

Liam set down his rucksack and wrapped his arms around me. "Be strong. I have faith in you, and I will always support you." He spoke very softly as he held me in his arms.

After that touching moment, he picked up his rucksack again and walked to the Chinooks. He boarded one, followed shortly by General Howard, who had no doubt gone in to debrief Liam and rest of his squad on the current mission, what they were to do when they arrived in Afghanistan, and a few side missions to gather enemy intelligence.

After General Howard had headed back to his office, I watched from afar as the Chinooks took off. To my surprise, Harry put his arm around me. I jumped a bit, as I had been deep in thought.

"I'm sorry about how distant I've been towards you. I just wanted to say that you will always have my support." He walked away as soon as he had said those words, disappearing before I had a chance to speak.

Girlie Bonding

After the Chinooks had taken off and Harry had pledged his support, I made my way to the mess hall to grab myself a coffee. I was about to sit down when Kirsten showed up, asking if I wanted to join her on a girls' night out. Once again, I recalled that party I had gone to with my high school friends.

Kirsten was doing everything she could to persuade me. I kind of agreed with her that this darkness was getting to me. *Just go for it*, I thought.

———◆✦◆———

Kirsten was excited that Scarlet had agreed to the girls' night out. When she'd first met Scarlet, she hadn't known what to think of her. But she could tell that Scarlet had been through a lot; and she'd thought she'd seen it all.

Kirsten was a fully qualified marine sniper who bragged to all the men. And she was a lesbian who had been let down by all the women in her life. Her father had mistreated her just because she was attracted to people of the same gender.

If there was one person in Kirsten's life who she despised most, it was her father. He was a fat, greedy pig of a man who always stole money from Kirsten's mother. He even stole Kirsten's pocket money, just so he could get booze down his throat and cigar nicotine into his lungs.

———◆✦◆———

After Kirsten convinced me to come with her on the girls' night, it was like a spark lit within her, telling her she could trust me. She told me about herself and her father, who she said was a total ass. She told me about the time she had given him a giant bruise on his eye, which he had hidden for months. But he had gotten his revenge and had broken her collarbone. If it weren't for her mother carefully taking pictures of the incident, Kirsten would never have shown them to the police and gotten her father busted.

I couldn't help but let out a few tears. I felt nothing but remorse and sorrow for her. I wrapped my arms around her.

Kirsten felt comfort in Scarlet's embrace. And to be honest, she felt something else as well. Scarlet was being so kind and caring. But she was lost in her own problems. All Kirsten could do was keep the promise she had made to Liam that she would look out for Scarlet.

Knowing Scarlet would support her as well felt good. The bond that developed from knowing they had each other's backs made them instant best friends.

Through the Mirror to Darkness

Kirsten and I had become really good friends. Tonight we were finally going out on the girls' night out she had been begging me to agree to for a while. At first I wasn't sure what to expect. I hadn't been out since that night when I had the hallucination of *her* watching me. Even now, I could still hear her whispering. My hands started to shake uncontrollably, and I felt sick.

I rushed to the restroom and went to the sink. I needed to cool down. But as soon as I lifted my head up, she was there—in the mirror.

I quickly turned around, trying not to acknowledge that she was there. "No!" I said. "No … you're not … real."

I could almost feel her burning with rage. Slowly, she reached out from the mirror. Before I knew what was happening, she had grabbed the front of my shirt and pulled me through the mirror.

I jumped to my feet. She was nowhere to be found. I even found a torch on the ground and pointed it in every direction. I looked behind me, and there was Nathaniel, extending his hand out to me. I bolted to him. But as I went to grab his hand, his body melted away into the darkness that took away his form.

My grip on the flashlight tightened. I felt so angry. Patches of darkness had started to fire at me. I aimed the torch's light at the dark missiles. As soon as the beam of light shined on the dark patches, they screeched in agony and faded away.

Suddenly, she appeared and put her hand on my shoulder. With the other hand, she handed me a 9mm pistol. The only thing I could think of was grabbing it and ending her for good. But when I shot at her, firing five times in succession, the bullets went straight through her, like I was trying to shoot a ghost.

I was worried. But then I shined the flashlight right in her face. I couldn't help but let out a slight smirk as the light from the flashlight scorched her. I stepped closer and closer to her until she was right below me. "I am done with you manipulating me," I said with anger in my voice.

To my surprise, Nathaniel grabbed my arm and looked deeply into my eyes. I met his gaze and held it, until he had slowly taken the gun out of my hands and dropped it on the pitch-black ground. He then placed both of his hands on my cheeks and wiped a single tear that was about to flow down my cheek, flicking the tear away with his thumb.

I tried to look behind me. But Nathaniel wouldn't let me. I had to fight him to get loose from his grip. He was a fully-grown version of himself, and he was really strong.

I grabbed hold of the flashlight that was holstered on the belt around my skinny jeans and flashed the light right in his eyes. Because it was the darkness that had created his adult form, the light burned and scorched his face.

"Ah!" he screamed. "How could you? Little sis! How could you?"

I tried not to feel guilty. All I could do was run away. I ran until I found myself back on the other side of the mirror. Looking down, I saw that the flashlight was still in my hand. Something was scratched into it—like a message of some sort. But I couldn't read it. I would soon find out what it meant—I hoped.

Two Girl's, One Darkness on a Friday Night

I looked at the clock. The time was still the same as it had been when I'd been grabbed and pulled into the mirror. It was almost like time had stopped. Then I realised I was supposed to meet Kirsten for our girls' night out. I quickly tied my hair into a bun. One side of my hair had a kind of messy look, so I brushed it back with my hands.

As I was walking to the car park, I bumped into Matthew. He already knew about our plans, seeing how Kirsten wasn't one to keep her mouth shut. I let out a giggle at his little joke about Kirsten.

As we went our separate ways, Matthew smiled at me in a way that suggested he couldn't help but smile.

When I met up with Kirsten a moment later, she smirked. "Matt has one helluva crush on you," she teased.

I put my hand on the back of my neck and smiled over my shoulder and then turned back to Kirsten. "I'm flattered, but I'm not ready for any relationship," I said giving her a half-smile.

"You need to have good time," Kirsten said playfully as we got in her car.

After an hour-long drive, we arrived at a club called Frisko's Disco. We were greeted by the owner of the club, Anderson Friskson. Kirsten greeted him like an old friend. As we entered the club, Anderson gave me a stern look with a hint of guile.

Kirsten quickly made her way to the bar. She came back in no time and handed me a glass. I was amazed how quickly she had ordered our drinks.

Before I knew it, it had been a couple of hours and, well, we'd had few—enough to make us completely tipsy. And with the loud progressive house music blasting out through the club's speakers, we couldn't help but get on the dance floor and boogie.

I immediately stopped dancing when my head began to pound from the stone-cold echoes of the Mistress of Darkness. When I got back to the table, I saw her just standing there, like she was nothing in particular—nothing more than a hallucination driven mad with frustration.

She might not have shown her frustration, but I could feel it. All she could do was stare at me from afar. Still, even when she couldn't come close, it was never easy for me. She was still manipulating me. I had no control whatsoever. No matter how strong I tried to be, my emotions were twisted—a part of my mind still centred on the notion that Nathaniel was in danger. Every time that thought would come up, I'd begin to feel more and more lost.

I found myself asking, *if* saving Nathaniel was possible, whether or not I could even do it. I mean, I'd never seen myself as a hero from a movie or a TV show. I could never see myself as a hero. To most people, I was a young woman with a problem. All I knew was that the darkness nibbled on my brain, bringing flashes of my childhood and filling them with dark thoughts.

As I sat at mine and Kirsten's table, I clenched my fists to stop my hands from trembling and also to keep my mind from falling deep into a dark slumber.

Kirsten stumbled over to me and snapped me out of the darkness.

She was too drunk to even understand that I was having hallucinations. I started to feel more human as she talked. Then she said something that stunned me speechless.

"I dare you to kiss me."

Her tone was quite serious, but due to the amount of alcohol she'd had, I figured she was joking. "Why do you want me to kiss you?" I asked.

———◆◆◆◆◆———

Kirsten took another sip of her drink. She had to make up a reason for having dared Scarlet to kiss her. The real reason was that she liked Scarlet. And she knew Scarlet liked her, but deep down she also knew it was not in the way she was thinking of.

All Kirsten could think of at that moment was what Scarlet's kiss would feel like. Would it be pure and gentle or rough and ravaging?

———◆◆◆◆◆———

I was still over Kirsten's, let's say, request. But she was drunk, so there might be a chance she wouldn't even remember anyway.

I took a sip from my beverage. Then I took a calming breath, placed my hands on her shoulders, and kissed her right on the lips.

———◆◆◆◆◆———

Kirsten was taken by surprise. The kiss left her head in the clouds. But also, while their lips we're pressed together, she had seen Scarlet's flashbacks and the Mistress of Darkness.

"Jesus Christ, you weren't kidding." Her drunkenness had been chased away by the middle-aged woman in a black ballgown looking at her and Scarlet.

Kirsten had been able to see everything that Scarlet had been seeing. But most importantly, Kirsten had seen Nathaniel—if she weren't a lesbian, she'd have a crush on him.

Kirsten pondered what to do to stop this. She had an idea. This time, it was her turn to kiss Scarlet.

Anderson the owner of the club watched the two girls from his office. His fat gut was telling him to report this mystery girl. But he'd wait for now.

I didn't have any say over it. But as soon as Kristen kissed me, the darkness inside me transferred back to me, leaving Kirsten even more curious. She demanded that Matthew and Harry should know what had happened.

Kirsten and I decided it was time to head home. Anderson Friskson appeared and stood in our way. He suggested we stay the night and offered us rooms. But I felt fine. I hadn't had as much to drink as I'd thought. So I simply declined.

He didn't seem too pleased. He never stopped watching us as we made our way to Kristen's car and headed out of the car park.

I headed along the route back to the barracks. Still the hallucinations never stopped. As I drove through the town leading up to the base, she was there watching me.

Though she was clearly still frustrated, she chuckled. It was as if she could see how desperate I had become—as if she believed I was now finally coming into her reach.

Chapter 4

Ransom

Kirsten Daydreams about Scarlet

The next morning, Kirsten awoke with a splitting headache. But one thing remained on her mind. The kiss from Scarlet stayed with her. That pure, sweet, gentle affection still felt hypnotic; it wasn't a normal kiss, like the kisses she'd had before. It was more magical.

And even though Kirsten had dared Scarlet to kiss her, she'd never expected it to be so hardcore. That's the way it had felt. In a way Kirsten felt bad. Matthew liked Scarlet, and it wouldn't be fair on him. Plus, it wouldn't be fair on Scarlet, 'cause she wasn't a lesbian; and the kiss probably didn't mean anything to her.

Sure it might have been a bundle of shits and giggles, just Scarlet humouring Kirsten. Scarlet had probably kissed her just as a friendly gesture. But how could a full-on kiss on the lips be a friendly gesture? Kirsten continued to ponder what the kiss might have meant. She placed her fingertips on her lips—she could almost still feel that hardcore affection.

Despite the uncertainty, over the next couple of days, Kirsten couldn't stop gushing. Scarlet was nothing like the women she'd thought she knew.

And it wasn't because she has this manipulating fear in her head. The truth was far from that.

Scarlet carried nothing but hope and optimism—like an aura. Kirsten couldn't help but admire her. No matter how weak she might be against this darkness, her kind heart, courageous attitude, loyalty, and honesty made her strong-willed.

Kirsten watched how Scarlet and Matthew would look at each other, and her jealousy made her feel stupid. But she never let the feeling of that kiss fade.

More importantly, since Scarlet had kissed her, Kirsten better understood all the flash visions Scarlet had been having. And she had seen the Mistress of Darkness.

Kirsten couldn't explain in detail what Scarlet's tormentor was, but she knew the mistress was a middle-aged woman in a black ballgown who tormented Scarlet's mind and twisted her emotions like she was a child's plaything.

Scarlet and the Darkness

That night made me feel so wrong. I knew, when I had kissed Kirsten, that my visions had transferred to her. I also knew that, as soon as Kirsten had kissed me back, they had gone straight back to me.

When we had gotten back to the apartments and I had made my way to my room, I had heard the Mistress of Darkness there. Her echoes were getting louder, and now she was threatening my friends. I was desperate to end this.

I was on my way to a debriefing about Liam's mission. The rumours about that hidden village he had been sent to were spreading like the latest story in a gossip magazine. Even new recruits like me knew they would be sent there if Liam and his squad failed.

Meanwhile, the Mistress of Darkness prowled like a lion around the base, wearing a sly smile. Luckily, no one but Scarlet could see her. To everyone else, she was invisible.

The mistress was finally getting the power she needed. Scarlet was getting desperate. And she had one more thing to push the girl over the edge. Not only could she dangle before her the chance to rescue Nathaniel from death. Now she also had the threat of her friends being in harm's way, in danger from the darkness. This would bring Scarlet to her knees.

She took it upon herself to track down Kirsten, Matthew, and Harry. The first two were easy to find.

Kirsten was telling Matthew what had happened during the girls' night out. Only she didn't say anything about the kiss. Instead, she made up something about what had allowed her to see Scarlet's visions.

Matthew was intrigued but horrified, thinking about what could come next. Would this darkness possibly come for them?

Before he could think too deeply about the possibilities, he felt a darkness come over his mind. The whole room went dark. And then nothing.

The Mistress of Darkness had slipped up behind Kirsten and Matthew. When she waved her hand over their eyes, the darkness had clouded their minds, sending them into a deep sleep. Only their eyes were still open.

With the wave of her hands, she had brought them to the dark place—to the other side of the world.

Now that she had captured Kirsten and Matthew, there was just Harry left. Lucky for Harry, he always kept out of the way. He was proving quite difficult to find.

Harry knew there was something up. After he checked the surveillance cameras, he had no doubt that something was going on. Kirsten and Matthew were standing like they were in zombie mode.

Harry had a pretty good guess as to what could be the cause. It was the darkness. It was probably using Kirsten and Matthew as bait for Scarlet.

Harry was terrified, but he knew he had to warn Scarlet. For now, though, he had to remain hidden. Being a veteran he'd had experience hiding from an enemy.

Scarlet in her Control

After the debriefing, I was greeted by Harry, who looked rather worried. He took me to the surveillance room. Luckily, he'd recorded the footage of Kirsten and Matthew.

I stared at the screen. The Mistress of Darkness was there. Unfortunately, Harry couldn't see her.

"Are you sure?" he exclaimed.

But before I could reply to Harry's question, I was knocked unconscious.

Harry was taken by surprise. He reached for his gun, but the Mistress of Darkness extended her hand to Harry's face. From her hand emerged a cloud of darkness that knocked him out cold.

She stood over the two, smirking. She was gloating. The time had come for the girl to make her stronger.

The pain in my head was crushing. My vision was blurred, and I couldn't even feel my hands. They were freezing cold; it felt like there was no circulation. I felt a certain chill in the air, and my body began to shiver. I started to wake up, except I felt laggy—like I wasn't in control of my own movements.

It wasn't until my eyes began to adjust and my vision focused on her that it came to me—I was now a puppet of the darkness.

Even though my body and part of my mind was hers, my thoughts were free. It felt like I was trapped in another body.

Then I saw Matthew, Kirsten, and Harry frozen in a cloud of darkness. My heart sank. Most of all, anger flared up in my veins. I was so frustrated that I was now her puppet; the only way I could move was by her command.

"Welcome to the darkness of trials, sweetheart."

She gloated and chuckled. This was what she had been waiting for since that night when I was ten years old—when she had first started appearing to me.

She gestured for me to walk towards her, and so I did. The darkness that clouded my mind seemed to have frozen my ability to control my body. I was nothing more than an empty shell.

She waved her hand in front of her, and a gust of darkness created a sort of round table in front of me. She calmly walked towards me and placed her hands on my shoulders. She waved her hand up, and the darkness created an image, kind of like a hologram but made of a cloud of darkness—an image of a woman.

She then leaned close to my ear and spoke in a whisper. "You see this lovely lady here?"

I nodded in reply.

"She was the one who took you away from your dear sweet mother."

All I could do was stare and wait for her order, but in my thoughts I was sickened by the request I sensed was coming—by what she wanted me to do.

"You want me to kill her," I said, my tone sounding serious and emotionless.

The Mistress of Darkness smirked and handed me a silenced sniper rifle, which I holstered on my back. She also holstered a silenced pistol on my belt. She then backed away. She raised her right hand and clicked her fingers—and a gust of darkness whisked me away to God knows where.

Trial 1: Quick and Clean

I was still under the control of the darkness. And clouds of darkness floated around me. I was well aware that, between the guns and the clouds, I must look like a mysterious demon assassinator. But even weirder still was that I was in a centre of a bustling town, but no one saw me. The pedestrians around me were walking through me like I was a ghost—like I wasn't here. I looked around and saw the cloud of darkness around me. Was the darkness protecting me?

But that wasn't important right now. My only concern was completing these trials so that I could save Nathaniel. I knew that she had him. I just knew it. But I couldn't worry about that now. What was more important was to track down this woman, who, surprisingly, was a social worker. I wasn't quite sure why the Mistress of Darkness wanted her dead.

I searched through a computer at a local library for social workers in the Seattle areas. The Mistress of Darkness gave a very vague description of what the woman I was to find looked like.

After searching for a couple of hours—during which I remained completely invisible to the locals—I finally found her. I had gone through a list of 159 social workers, but I had found her.

Her name was Cynthia King. She matched the mistress's description. A part of me felt wrong about all this. It was like I was playing the part of darkness's personal hit man.

I then downloaded the information to my phone so I could track down this woman. She was somewhere around the suburbs in Vancouver, BC, Canada. As soon as the downloading finished, I took off to the train station and hitched a ride to Vancouver. I couldn't imagine what I was gonna do to this woman as I glanced at the silenced sniper rifle holstered to my back. I had another holster on my belt, which held a silenced pistol.

During the train ride, I could hear the whispers in my head, not so much from the Mistress of Darkness but from my past. I heard the care workers' voices, and the voices of the other kids in the children's home. And then there was Nathaniel's voice, which was somewhat louder than the other voices. George and Nicole's voices began to echo in the background, too along with those of Conner, Jodie, Toby, and even Liam.

Hearing the voices made me feel faint. I began to feel barely conscious. The darkness that was controlling me felt like it was fading away from my mind, like it couldn't take the pressure from head. But it was never gonna let me go. Even if it did, I needed to complete these trials. I had to. I had to do it to save Nathaniel.

After the train journey, I entered Cynthia King's address into my phone's mapping app. I walked around, looking at my phone for directions. That was when I stumbled upon an abandoned car in a shadowed alleyway.

My curiosity was growing. And I had to admit, it would be a lot easier to get around in a car. I wasn't sure if it was the darkness in me talking, seeing how my thoughts were free. I ended up pausing a lot, but the darkness wouldn't let me. And I couldn't abandon these trials. I would do anything to save Nathaniel—even if it killed me.

It was midnight when I made it to a peaceful little suburban village. It wasn't long until I found the correct address. It looked like one of those old-fashioned cottages you'd normally see in the countryside. But I didn't have time to wonder about the architecture. I had a trial to complete.

I made my way to the front door and picked the lock with a bobby pin. When the door opened, I had to be careful of the hulking Rottweiler in front of me. I wasn't sure about this situation. Sure, humans couldn't see me, but it was the animals I was worried about. After all, animals had far better senses than humans.

So I sneaked quietly up the stairs, the silenced pistol in my hand. I had started to feel nervous. My hands wouldn't stop shaking. I almost wanted to back out of this.

But I knew I couldn't. That didn't stop my hands shaking—even as I opened the doors to find this Cynthia King.

She was sleeping, not realising what was about to happen. Her husband was sleeping next to her. I began to tear up as I pressed the gun to her forehead and looked away; the tears were flowing down my face.

As soon as I pulled the trigger, I glanced at her. I felt sick. I collapsed to my hands and knees and cried out my sorrow. The darkness whisked me away before her husband had awoken, and the hulking Rottweiler downstairs came barking up the stairs.

Mr King Mourns His Wife

After I was whisked away by the darkness, Mr King shot up from his slumber. Turning on his light, he saw his dear wife Cynthia lying beside him. The colour had completely drained from her face. Blood from the bullet wound had painted the pillow red. Her husband held her in his arms as he cried deeply from his heart.

He reached for his phone and called the local law enforcement and the ambulance. Mr King could barely talk through the pain of his broken heart.

It wasn't long till the ambulance had arrived. The EMTs grabbed their gear and ran up the stairs to tend to the emergency.

When Mr King saw their faces, he began to break down. There was nothing they could do. The bullet had entered her skull between her eyes. Hers had been an instant death. It wasn't long till the police arrived and the paramedics removed Cynthia from the house.

Mr King was then questioned by one of the officers, while the other officers looked for any clues. They searched and searched the residence but were unable to find so much as a trace of a lead. One of the officers decided to call in a dog unit.

Meanwhile, the officer who was questioning Mr King was beginning to get annoyed. He was getting nowhere, due to the fact that Mr King kept breaking down and weeping inconsolably. Of course the officer understood that Mr King's wife had been murdered. He knew what loss was, since he had experienced something similar.

"Why?!" Mr King cried. "How …? How could someone do this? Cynthia never did anything wrong to anyone. Yeah, she had her disagreements with some people. But nobody would want her dead." He covered his face with his hands, his shoulders shaking.

It wasn't long until an officer showed up with her canine companion—Officer Layton and her five-year-old spaniel, Jesse.

Officer Layton got out the car and headed to the boot where Jesse was. As she opened the door, the dog's tailed wagged uncontrollably and she let out an excited moan. Layton clipped the lead on Jesse's collar, and in the house they went, Jesse pulling the lead with excitement.

Jesse the Dog

After Officer Layton got a debriefing on the situation, Mr King was told to take his Rottweiler away from the crime scene, so the hyperactive spaniel could do her job.

As soon as Officer Layton let the dog off the lead, she began sniffing for a scent. Jesse's brain was processing every scent in the house.

But there was another smell—a wrong smell. This is scent was alien enough for the sniffer dog to be stopped in her tracks. She had been trained to sniff out many types of substances—drugs, money, explosives, and firearms. But she had never come across anything like this scent.

Officer Layton was about to give up, seeing how Jesse wasn't getting a direct scent. Yet Jesse had a good reputation of sniffing out anything that could be found. She also had a proud family background, as both her mom and dad were excellent police dogs as well.

Mr King was anxious as he walked in and watched the spaniel still sniffing. When Jesse sniffed the spot right next to the side of the bed where Cynthia King had been shot, she stopped.

There was something there. But the scent smelt wrong. It was there, but then it wasn't. Jesse let out a slight moan as she pawed at the ground with her front paw.

The officers, including Officer Layton went to the spot Jesse had been pawing at.

One of the officer's placed his finger on the piece of carpet, and it felt weird. The officer couldn't describe it. It was like the carpet was simultaneously all dried up and moist—kind of like the suspect had vanished into thin air.

As Jesse continued to sniff the carpet, a light growl escaped from her throat. She moaned again and pawed at the ground with her feathery paws.

The light began to flicker, which confused Officer Layton, the other officers, and Mr King. The spaniel began to growl deep in her throat again. Blind animal terror pierced her brain. She knew something was wrong—very wrong.

Harry Released from the Darkness

I had returned to the place of darkness. I still felt wrong about having pulled the trigger and killing Cynthia King. The Mistress of Darkness came out of the shadows and clapped a gentle hand on my shoulder. I instantly pushed her away.

Surprised, I paused and looked around me. It seemed the darkness didn't possess me while I was here. Instead, I was handcuffed by a cloud of darkness.

At first, the Mistress of Darkness was taken aback. But then she placed her hand on my chin and made me look into her eyes. "Fine," she snarled. "You wanna keep on hating me, then keep on hating me."

She smirked when I spat in her face. She wiped the spittle from her cheek with her finger and put her finger in her mouth, smirking again as she tasted it.

"Since you completed the first trial, one of your friends will earn their freedom." She pointed to my friends. "The catch is, you have to choose who you want to go free."

A part of me couldn't think straight, seeing how the darkness had been in control of my body and parts of my mind. It left me feeling weak and groggy. I looked towards Matthew, Kirsten, and Harry. See them being held hostage by this darkness was so upsetting.

The Mistress of Darkness was beginning to get frustrated with my hesitation. She threatened to kill one of them if I didn't make a decision. So I pondered for a bit and decided to let Harry go free first. I could only hope that his memory would be intact and that he'd try and figure out a way to rescue Kirsten and Matthew. Or perhaps he would be able to track my every move when I continued these trials.

She kept her promise and let Harry go. All of a sudden, a gust of darkness circled around me, and through it, I watched him fade back to where he had come from.

<hr />

Harry awoke gasping for breath. He tried to remember what had happened. But there was nothing there. There seemed to be a blank spot in his mind.

There was one thing he did know, though. Scarlet was in trouble. So he started hacking as best he could, pouring through surveillance footage from the local area and surrounding states.

Trial 2: Silence and Stealth

After Harry was freed, I stared at Matthew and Kirsten, who were still cryogenically frozen in clouds of darkness.

Suddenly she was using her magic darkness to control me again. She gestured for me to come forward.

Again my body and part of my mind was in her control. This time my head ached painful. The Mistress of Darkness used her darkness to create new forms—this time, three people were shaped out of the cloud of darkness.

The Mistress of Darkness explained that these people were care workers who had worked at the children's home where Nathaniel and I had been sent. I slowly turned my head to face the Mistress of Darkness. She was giving me a sly smile.

"You want me to hunt them down and eliminate them," I heard myself saying.

The mistress's smile grew wider; she looked pleased with my answer.

"Only this time, I won't be able to protect you from being seen. You're gonna have to be careful and leave no evidence of your presence."

After she said this, she gave me a cloak to help me keep out of sight.

Then all of a sudden, a gust of darkness had whisked me back to civilisation.

I found myself in a shadowed alleyway. Before I stepped out of the alley, I put the cloak on and lifted the hood over my head. I wanted to be sure people couldn't detect my facial features if this plan went horribly wrong.

I mostly stuck to the shadows, since I wasn't being protected by the darkness this time. I thought my task was to find a good source of information. My memories were vague. The best place to start my search was the orphanage where Nathaniel and I had been sent back in Seattle.

The Mistress of Darkness started to speak to me, her words ice cold in my mind. "Head over to Avenue Square car park," she instructed. "Something there will help you reach your destination."

After she spoke, a gust of darkness blew, and in my possession was a set of car keys. "At least I won't have to board a train this time," I muttered.

Walking along the dark street, and I'm gonna be honest here, was pretty scary. I may have been possessed by the darkness, but the fear of getting ganged up on and mugged or even worse was strong. The possibilities were terrifying just to think about.

I finally made my way to the car park. It was jam-packed with cars. I pondered which one I was intended to find. Then an idea occurred to me. I lifted the keys above my head and pressed the buttons until the lights on a black Aston Martin flashed repeatedly. I was at first taken aback by this turn of events. This was a fancy car, not very discreet. But I couldn't think about it now. I had three care workers to deal with.

When I got in the driver's seat, the dashboard flickered with darkness. Slowly, I extended my hand and inside I found a GPS. I placed it on the stand. As soon as my finger made contact with the screen, the mistress's voice came from it. She gave me more information about the three care workers I was to find.

Nathan Deagan, Anita Shaw, and Cheryl Pembroke were their names. Looking back in my mind, I remembered that, on the day Nathaniel had died, Cheryl Pembroke had been there. In fact, she was always there for me. Whenever I would lock myself in my room, I always let her in. She'd tell me stories and say that, no matter where Nathaniel was, he would always be watching over me.

I turned the key in the ignition, and off I went, following the GPS to the children's home in Seattle.

After a couple of hours of driving, I arrived at the children's home. My memory was good, and I recognised the building. I parked the car in a dark abandoned alleyway and walked towards the home.

I used one of my bobby pins to open the door. Luckily, there was no one in sight, I slowly crept in and entered the office. I wasted no time and immediately started searching for the whereabouts of Anita, Nathan, and Cheryl.

Luckily, Nathan and Cheryl were still here. In fact, they were both in the building now. I had to think of a quick, silent death. An idea came to me. I crept into the kitchen and found a large sharp knife.

I carefully walked to Cheryl's room. There she was. She looked the same as I remembered—still pretty. Tears flowed down my cheek as I found some duct tape and carefully taped it over her mouth. She stirred but didn't awake immediately.

At first I couldn't do it. My guilt over killing Cynthia King had crept back into my mind. Now I was imagining the emotions I would end up feeling after this.

I shook my head and focused on my task. I pressed the knife against Cheryl's neck and slowly slit her throat. Her eyes flew open in shock. Blood poured from her neck. She died quickly.

Cheryl's blood made me sick to my stomach. The foul stench pierced my nose. I dropped to my knees, and my hands began to shake uncontrollably.

The knife in my hand felt heavy as I clutched it deep into the palm of my hand.

I then made my way to Nathan's room. I stumbled in. My legs felt like jelly. I could barely stand on my own two feet. I trembled, holding the silenced pistol in my hand. I pointed the barrel of the pistol towards Nathan's head. I turned my head away, clenched my eyes shut, and pulled the trigger. Just like with Cynthia King, the bullet killed him instantly.

The sickly feeling made me want to faint. Pinpoints of sweat dripped down my face, which I knew was pale and ill-looking.

A gust of darkness took the knife away, snapping me back to attention. I quickly stumbled out of the care home and disappeared into the darkness, rushing back to the car.

I barely felt conscious. My hands still trembled uncontrollably, I wasn't sure if this was a side effect of the darkness or of the guilt of having committed murder.

On top of that memories of my time at the care home filled my brain, and Nathaniel's voiced echoed in my ears, piercing my heart. I couldn't think about that right now. I punched Anita Shaw's address into the GPS system.

Her residence was in the suburbs of Seattle, not far from the care home. I wasted no time getting there. I needed to complete these trials so I could save my friends and, most importantly, save Nathaniel.

I found the house I was looking for tucked into the peaceful suburbs of Seattle. Just like I had at the care home, I parked the car in the nearby woods, slipping it in behind some trees and made my way to Anita's house. Instead of breaking in the front, I decided to creep in through the back. I gripped the silenced pistol in the palm of my hand. To my surprise, the back door was open for some reason.

As soon as I opened the back door a crack, I could tell somebody was already up, I quietly crouched, waiting to see who it was. Luckily for me, this was my last target for this trial.

Anita Shaw was a lonely widow who had lost her husband to an aggressive form of brain cancer not long ago. Her adopted son had been killed in Afghanistan a couple of years before her husband's death.

I stood behind her as she held a picture frame with a photo of her husband and son to her chest, her eyes gently closed. I used the silenced pistol to knock her out cold. I then bent down and pressed the barrel against her head. I looked away and closed my eyes tightly as I pulled the trigger.

I took a peek at the body of Anita. My hands trembled and I felt sick and dizzy. I had no opportunity to react any further. The darkness, as it had before, whisked me away from the scene.

The second trial was now complete.

Children in a Home Alone

The sun had risen, and the children were about wake up. One little girl had come down stairs to the kitchen. To her surprise, no adult was in sight. Instead of alerting the others, she decided to look for Nathan and Cheryl first.

To the little girl's horror, she found the two care workers and screamed in terror. The sight of the blood and their limp bodies terrified and upset her.

The other children heard the ear-splitting scream. The two oldest children quickly bolted down the stairs, followed by the rest of them. When they laid their eyes on the bodies of Nathan and Cheryl, nothing but fear impaled their minds.

The youngest of the group burst into tears. It wasn't just that the children were scared. They were looking at the bodies of the only two adults they had known who were like family to them. Their little hearts were broken. The kids started to panic.

The oldest girl went into the office and called the police.

The children never left the care workers' sides, even when the paramedics rushed in and declared officially that there was nothing they could do. Nathan and Cheryl were dead.

It wasn't long until the police had arrived. One of the officers called in social workers to remove the children from the premises. It wasn't easy for the police to remove them, since they were mourning the deaths of their care workers. What made it worse was that it was clear that the younger ones were too young to fully understand what was going on.

The two oldest were questioned, but to no avail. The children hadn't seen or heard anything. This felt like a dead end for the police.

One officer suggested they call in Officer Layton and her canine companion. If there was one nose to sniff out who had this it would be that canine.

It wasn't long until the social workers arrived and escorted the children out. As all of them were traumatised, none of them hesitated to get out of there. The officers remained on the scene, waiting for Officer Layton to arrive.

Something in the Air

A couple of hours after the children left the premises with the social workers, Officer Layton arrived. Before she got her canine companion out of the car, one of the officers debriefed her on the situation. Something about it made Officer Layton think of the recent murder of Cynthia King.

As she got the spaniel out of the vehicle, the dog let out a joyous bark. Her tail wagged uncontrollably with excitement as she jumped out and pulled her handler into the building.

The officers had struck out. Whoever had committed this murder had known exactly what he or she was doing and left no visible signs of evidence. To be honest, it scared the shit out of them.

As soon as Officer Layton let the dog off the lead, the canine began searching. Every scent the dog inhaled caused a pinprick of fear in the dog's brain.

"Something doesn't feel right," Officer Layton said softly. Goosebumps had formed on her neck. She shivered. The air suddenly felt cold and almost kind of moist.

The spaniel could sense Officer Layton and the other officers' fear. She whimpered, and her brown eyes stared at her handler.

Officer Layton chose to ignore the weird sensation. Since Jesse was getting distracted, she got her four-legged friend back on track. The spaniel continued sniffing the area.

While the spaniel searched the rooms, one of the officers got another call-out to another murder. After the officer got the debriefing, she requested that Officer Layton come along too.

Officer Layton agreed. As she was about to put Jesse on the lead, the lights began to flicker and the air became cold and moist again.

One of the officers pulled his 9mm pistol out of its holster and, frustrated, stumbled into the room. "Enough of this paranormal horseshit," he yelled. Then he began shooting around, all the while shouting inappropriate language.

Officer Layton and the other two officers ducked out of his line of fire. Officer Layton confronted him and snatched his gun out of his hand, speaking very sternly to him

Insulted, the officer let out an angry outburst.

"Hey, muzzle discipline," Officer Layton said, holding her hand in front of the officer's face.

He he pushed her aside and stormed out of the building, reaching for his cigarettes and lighter.

Officer Layton turned back to the other two officers. She made her way to her canine companion and attached the leash on the dog's collar. The officers waited until she exited the building before placing police tape on the doors and around the front entrance to the orphanage.

Officer Layton's Thoughts

On her way to the next call-out, Officer Layton contemplated what had happened at the last two crime scenes. She couldn't grasp these murders; it seemed like someone was using paranormal dark forces to commit. But the theory sounded completely ridiculous.

Still, something strange was going on. That theory could at least account for a few things. It would explain why Jesse appeared to be clueless, unable to pick up the slight bit of scent on the scene.

But Officer Layton didn't jump to conclusions. It was a promising theory, but that's all she kept it as—a theory.

The only other question she was asking was why. Why would someone commit these murders? What was this person's agenda? To Layton, the murders didn't seem random. Plus, unlike some of her colleagues, who seemed to take their jobs to find a suspect right away a bit too seriously, Officer Layton didn't like to point fingers at potential suspects, not until she had all the facts.

Layton's canine companion was getting excited. The dog's tail began to wag uncontrollably, and she started to paw her cage and moan excitedly.

The journey wasn't that far. But due to the amount of traffic on the roads, it took another hour to get to the next call-out. While she was stationary in traffic she had an idea—she could contact an old friend. He was a CIA field agent who had previously been a forensics researcher with the FBI, and he had a knack for hacking through surveillance and computer programming. Layton connected her phone to the monitor and searched for her friend's number in her contacts.

No matter how many times she called, the call rang and rang until the voicemail message picked up. Officer Layton was getting anxious. It had been awhile since they last spoke, but she knew Matthew would never ignore his phone calls.

Something strange is going on, she thought. She and Matthew Tyran still kept in touch through Facebook.

This week had *strange* written all over it, and it scared the living shit out of her. She was going in blind, with only her theory and her thoughts.

The slow-moving traffic started to pick up. Layton was anxious. What gruesome scene would she find this time?

Harry Hacks Around

Harry hadn't left the surveillance room since he'd been freed from the darkness. He was searching surveillance footage and trying to hack security cameras all around the States. Harry wasn't gonna lie; hacking wasn't his best skill. He wasn't like Matthew; that guy could hack his way into a secret enemy base and gather enemy intelligence without anyone even knowing he was there.

But right now, all he could do was keep searching and just hope and pray that Scarlet and the others were okay. Knowing what was out there and what Scarlet's psychotic episodes were like made him shiver.

<hr>

General Howard trusted Harry, but he hadn't seen or heard from him. On top of that, he hadn't seen Miss Jayden or those other two who stuck to her like glue.

Something didn't seem right this week. The media was blowing up because of these mysterious murders. The law enforcement teams involved in the cases were annoyed that the press had stuck its noses in official business, and they were frustrated because the murders had left them scrambling. Something was up.

⬥•⬥✕⬥•⬥

Harry became suspicious. He too had been thinking of the murders. The reporters called it anonymous slaughter. The police refused to weigh in on the case with the press, annoyed the media was nosing around.

Suddenly, Harry's train of thought was interrupted by General Howard, who seemed a bit more tense then usual.

"Is there a problem, sir?" Harry jumped to his feet and stood behind the chair, looking a bit nervous. Throughout the conversation, he glanced at the monitors whenever General Howard didn't seem to be paying much attention.

"Local law enforcement has been requesting our help with these murders. Do you think you could contact the DCST?" General Howard snapped, his tone filled with displeasure.

Harry knew General Howard was a hard-ass, but his attitude seemed a bit more extreme than normal. "Why can't someone in the FBI profile division contact the DC Swat Team?" he asked, curious.

General Howard explained that the others had their own assigned duties and that Harry was the only one who was off duty.

Harry felt torn. He wanted to use the surveillance monitors to find Scarlet and the others. Now he had to focus on the SWAT team and the murder investigations. He would feel guilty if things with his friends and squad mates turned sour.

A Murder Not Deserved

A couple hours after Scarlet had killed Anita Shaw and been whisked away by the darkness, a neighbour of Mrs Shaw's arrived to deliver her milk and her newspaper. When she went to open the door, the neighbour felt a hint of suspicion. Anita unlocked her front door at eight o'clock every morning. But the door was locked.

Her neighbour noticed the gate to the backyard was open. This raised another suspicion. She walked to the back door, which, also strangely, was open. She walked slowly and steadily inside and called out to Anita.

On entering the living room, she was confronted with a horrible vision. There lay Anita Shaw on the floor, blood dripping from her forehead. Unable to bear the gruesome sight, the neighbour bolted past the body and straight to the telephone. She called for an ambulance and the police.

It wasn't long until the police arrived, with Officer Layton in tow. As soon as they entered the household, Anita's body confirmed what they knew; she was already dead.

Officer Layton and another of the officers questioned the neighbour about Mrs Shaw.

Something told Officer Layton that this wasn't a coincidence—that the same person or the same thing had killed Mrs King and those two care workers, Mr Deagan and Ms Pembroke. And whoever or whatever it was had killed Anita Shaw as well.

"I normally come every morning to deliverer Anita's milk and newspaper," the neighbour was saying. "She never leaves her property, not since she lost her husband four months ago. She also lost her son two years ago."

A few minutes later, the ambulance arrived to remove the body of Anita Shaw. Officer Layton, as usual, led her canine companion, Jesse, into the house. Meanwhile she continued thinking about all that it happened and praying that there would be some kind of lead.

Officer Layton let the dog off the lead, and no sooner had the little spaniel stared sniffing than she darted to a spot on the floor. The dog's tail begins to wag uncontrollably.

Officer Layton guided the canine where to sniff, leading her to a spot near the doorway next to the armchair.

The dog stopped dead. Her tail halted. And she stared directly at one particular spot.

Layton took point and investigated what Jesse had found. What she discovered took her by surprise. "It's a 9mm bullet," she exclaimed, examining the bullet closely.

She saw that some sort of indecipherable lettering had been imprinted on it. Layton was intrigued. Eagerly, she requested that the officers take the bullet to the lab and have it analysed.

After the officers left, Layton offered a tennis ball to her canine companion as reward. As she breathed in ease, a glimpse of hope was sparked inside Officer Layton. For now, all she could do was keep her fingers crossed and hope that they would find this mysterious murderer.

Matthew Released from the Darkness

Back in the dark place, the Mistress of Darkness could feel the power of the trial's completion rushing through her. The power that the darkness was longing for was finally here. Its desire for power was truly extraordinary. Now she finally had the girl in the palm of her hands, and she embraced the powerful feeling.

A sly smile spread across her face as the girl appeared before her.

As soon as I arrived back in the dark place, I fell on my hands and knees in remorse. the guilt was tearing me apart.

"Please!" I screamed. "Don't make me do this!" I clenched my fists, trying to regain my strength.

The Mistress of Darkness looked down upon me. She wielded her superiority in this dark place over me, and I hated her for it. I glared deeply into her eyes. But the pain the darkness had left me in was so intense it felt like my body was being ripped apart. That's when she used her cloud of darkness to float me up onto my feet. But the moment my feet made contact with ground, my legs gave way instantly.

The Mistress of Darkness turned towards me and gloated. The smug smile remained on her face as she uncrossed her arms and knelt down next to me. She lifted up my chin until I was forced to make eye contact with her.

"How does it feel to suffer in pain?" she asked. Then pressing her face so close to mine we were nearly touching, she added, "Painful isn't it? Now you know how she must have felt." Looking at me with sharp eyes, she continued to gloat at my weakening state.

My muscles burned, and my joints ached. I could barely feel anything but endless pain. I wonder what she had done to me while I was under the control of the darkness.

Before she could ask who I would free next, it occurred to me that I still had my little bag. It was a long shot, but I had to try. I reached inside, and to my surprise, the flashlight that had come into my possession, was still there. Ignoring my pain, I pulled out the flashlight and beamed it at the clouds of darkness holding Matthew and Kirsten suspended in the air.

The darkness screeched in pain, and both Matthew and Kirsten collapsed to the dark non-existent floor. I scrambled to them. Their breathing was dangerously heavy, but they were alive.

I got myself into a defensive position to protect Matthew and Kirsten and shined the flashlight towards the Mistress of Darkness. Somehow, she managed to shield herself from the light's harm.

"Disobeying orders, are we?" She cackled and then extended her hands towards me.

Instantly, a gust of darkness blew me back, knocking me right off my feet.

The Mistress of Darkness walked slowly towards me with her arms crossed. But as she got to Matthew and Kirsten, she waved her hand. The darkness whisked Matthew away, and Kirsten was put back in suspension.

"I admire your courage, but you are far too weak and mindless to stop me." She extended her hands again. Just like before, the gust of darkness blew me back, knocking the flashlight to the ground.

I grabbed for it, but the mistress stepped on my hand. The pressure from her heel was intense. I winced in agony and begged her to stop.

◆◆◆

Matthew woke up back at the base. He quickly jumped up, trying to remember what had happened. But everything was a blur. He knew there was one thing he had to do; he had to find Scarlet and the others.

◆◆◆

Harry saw Matthew on the surveillance camera. He bolted from the security room to catch up with him.

A Boys' Debriefing

Harry finally caught up to Matthew, who was still feeling the affects from being released from the darkness. Harry took him aside and pulled him into the security room He explained what had being going on and showed him the video footage he'd saved of when Matthew and Kirsten had been taken.

"What the hell is happening?" Matthew was completely confused by what he had just seen.

Harry informed him that Scarlet had told him this Mistress of Darkness from her visions was responsible.

"Why?" Matthew asked.

Harry wasn't sure, so he couldn't give Matthew a clear answer. But what he did say shocked Matthew right to the core. "I think this Mistress of Darkness that Scarlet keeps talking about is somehow using us as bait to get to Scarlet."

Matthew felt horrible. The thought of Scarlet being used as the devil's plaything and himself being used to make that happen made him feel sick to his stomach. "There must be something we can do," he said, desperate for a response.

Harry couldn't say, since he had woken up with no memory of what had happened and no idea who had committed the murders being reported by the local medias.

Matthew hadn't been in the security room for long when his phone started vibrating. He took out his phone and looked at screen in surprise.

An old friend's name had appeared on the screen. And apparently she'd called a number of times. "Lydia?" Matthew said quietly, confused as to why she would need to reach him so urgently.

Matthew listened to the voice message Lydia Layton had left him.

Layton needed his expert hacking skills to locate the murderer everyone was speculating about. She wanted him to use the CFA's security systems.

Matthew explained to Harry what the voice message was all about. Harry explained that he'd been doing the best he could to hack through the base's security systems and to scan the footage of the CCTV cameras across all the states.

"What if we locate Scarlet?" said a very anxious Matthew as he looked at Harry and then glanced back to his phone.

Harry couldn't say anything. He'd poured all his loyalty into helping his squad mates back when he'd served his first mission with the navy. Now because of General Howard's approval, he'd earned a place in the CFA and the rank of lieutenant.

Matthew felt torn. He'd never had many friends. His relationship with Lydia was never anything romantic. She was more like a big sister to him than anything, but it was as far as loyalty had gone with him back in Phoenix.

That was until he'd first met Kirsten. They'd been close ever since they were assigned to work together on an operation that involved his knack with hacking security systems and Kirsten's trusty sniping kills—which had earned her several ranks and medals for highest kill counts, along with her place with the CFA.

Matthew had had several choices after he'd received his own medals. He could have stayed with the FBI, which would have gained him the rank of a profiler. Instead, he had chosen to join the CIA as a field agent. He'd made this decision so he wouldn't have to go back home to his family, since he had never gotten on with his stepmother.

Then after working in the CIA as a novice field agent for a few months, he had been offered a place in the CFA. At first, he'd hesitated. But he'd accepted the opportunity after he had earned the rank of chief field agent.

Trial 3: Trial by Fire

I awoke in sheer agony. I had been numb and was filled with pain. My vision wasn't yet clear again. My hands and feet felt like ice chunk. I could barely even feel them. It wasn't long until I realised I was handcuffed by a cloud of darkness, which would explain why I felt so cold—the coldness was like that in the Arctic.

The sheer agonising pain was like being stabbed by a thousand knives. The Mistress of Darkness gloated as she used her cloud of darkness to levitate me off the ground to her round table of darkness.

"There is one more thing we need to do before we leave Seattle." She paused for a bit before she waved her right hand. And the care home I was at when I was a kid appeared on her round table of darkness.

"Please! Don't make me do this," I cried out in pain.

She turned and grabbed my chin so I could see her eye-to-eye. "Don't worry, sweetheart!" she said in an icy tone. "This time I'm coming with you."

No sooner had she spoken than she let me go. In my weak state, I was unable to stand on my own two legs, so I collapsed to the freezing darkness-filled ground.

The Mistress of Darkness then turned herself into a cloud of darkness and inhaled herself inside me.

The sensation of her presence was agonising, maybe even worse than the pain I was already in. I instantly dropped to my knees as she adjusted herself inside of me.

After that, I felt nothing, just cold darkness. I felt like a stranger in my own body. The Mistress of Darkness was now in full control.

I was whisked away, and I was back in the same place where I had killed Anita Shaw. Police tape surrounded the house's entrance. Though my sorrow remained in my thoughts, I was now being fully controlled. Under this power, I climbed into the Aston Martin I had hidden in the woods near Anita's house.

As I drove, something in the glove compartment was making a racket. I opened the compartment. What I saw made me pull over. There in the compartment was a satchel filled with C-4 and a detonator.

In sheer terror, I dropped the satchel. I struggled to regain control of my own actions. The Mistress of Darkness instantly asserted her control. She didn't take kindly to me fighting back. My body felt clenched buy her presence, as if she was digging her fingernails into my brain.

As soon as I started the car back up, I made my way back to the orphanage. I knew what she wanted me to do when I got there; she wanted me to burn the orphanage to the ground.

When I arrived at the orphanage, I saw police tape surrounding the entrance, just like at Anita Shaw's house. I couldn't help but feel partly responsible, even though I had been under control of the darkness. If I got caught by the law, there would be no excuse of darkness manipulating me. I'd be branded as crazy, and I would probably be committed to a mental asylum.

After I parked the car in an abandoned, shadowy alleyway, I grabbed the satchel containing the C-4 and attached the detonator to my belt. I walked casually towards the orphanage, and the Aston Martin faded away into darkness.

With the front entrance completely closed up, I decided to climb through the back window leading to the kitchen. I remembered that window always stayed open.

As soon as I entered, I was filled with nostalgia. Memories flooded into my mind. And then there was the memory of that tragic day.

That day had haunted me to this day. I felt remorse but also hope. I though to myself, *I promise I'll bring you back, big brother.*

After I had planted all of the C-4 in every angle of the building, something caught my eye on the orphanage notice board. It was a group photo from back when Nathaniel and I were there. It must have been taken not long before we were to be fostered. As I studied the photo more closely, I realised it was taken on the day before the accident.

With the C-4 planted, I bolted out through the window and took cover within the trees in the back garden, behind the tree house. Slowly, I pulled out the detonator. Closing my eyes, I aimed the detonator at the building. "I'm sorry," I said quietly as I pulled the trigger. The building lit up and burst into flames.

———◆◆✕◆◆———

Officer Layton arrived on the scene at the orphanage. She had been nearby and had seen the blast. Shielding her eyes from the bright flames, she radioed for backup, telling the dispatch to send the fire department. Then she ran towards the building she had investigated earlier.

———◆◆✕◆◆———

I was still hiding in the trees when female officer rounded the corner and came towards the gardens. She pulled out her flashlight, scanning the area. The beam of light flashed on me. With the darkness possessing me, the light painfully burned my skin.

"Hey!" the officer screamed. "*You*! Stop right there!"

I bolted away, keenly aware she was chasing after me.

Layton Chases Scarlet

The mysterious figure had made a run for it, but Officer Layton refused to let this person get away. She chased after the person who had been hiding behind of the orphanage.

"I am giving chase to an unknown witness at the crime location," Officer Layton said into her police radio as she ran towards the fleeing figure.

The person knocked over bins to slow her down. Layton jumped over them dodging left and right and sliding over car bonnets.

Scarlet could not outrun the cop, as she was one determined woman. Scarlet had to think how to lose her. She decided to take a bit of a detour and climbed up a window cleaner's ladder.

With the window cleaner still on the ladder, Scarlet had to jump halfway up the ladder to get on top of the roof.

That didn't stop her pursuer. The officer was right on her tail. Suddenly, Scarlet felt herself being grabbed by the waist. And then she landed on top of a vehicle.

The woman Officer Layton had finally managed to tackle threw a few punches once they'd both gotten to their feet. But Officer Layton was a skilled fighter. As a child, she had been a black belt in jiu-jistsu. That combined with her police training made her a force to be reckoned with.

While fighting, Layton couldn't make out what this woman looked like. Whoever she was, she wore a hood that covered most of her face. That and the fact that she was getting her ass kicked prevented her from getting a good look at her assailant; she was impressed at this anonymous woman's hand-to-hand combat skills.

Officer Layton was about to grab her baton, but the woman grabbed it out of her holster and started using it as an advantage. A blow to the head and then a whack to her back knocked her to the ground.

Officer Layton slowly got up. She saw that her baton was lying on the ground next to her. She grabbed it and holstered it. She looked everywhere for the anonymous woman. But her assailant seemed to have disappeared into the night.

She asked all the pedestrians in the area. But it was a dead end. No one had seen the woman.

Officer Layton radioed her team. "The potential suspect got away. I repeat the potential suspect has gotten away. Making my way back now," she reported as she walked back to her car.

A Break in Trial

As soon as the officer I'd been fighting with had fallen to the ground, the darkness has whisked me away. When I got back to the dark place, the Mistress of Darkness released herself from me, which left me in a critical state. I couldn't feel my legs. I dropped to the ice-cold dark floor.

"Now that was quite enjoyable. Don't you think?" She sounded quite thrilled, and she continued to smirk.

I tried to stand up but to no avail. It seemed the weaker I got, the stronger she became. I was desperate to find a way out of here. I looked up toward Kirsten, who remained frozen in darkness.

I noticed the torch, but the Mistress of Darkness had hold of me with her cloud of darkness once again. I struggled through the cloud to get free from her clutches, but she had me with a firm grip, making it impossible to wriggle free.

"Please. I thought you'd help me save … Nathaniel!" I spoke forcefully, trying to ignore how much pain I was in.

She gestured for her cloud of darkness to bring me closer—right in her face.

I was literally eye to eye with her. We were so close that I could even smell her perfume, which somehow seemed familiar to me. It was like I knew somebody who wore that same perfume. I stared deeply into her eyes.

"Now, now my dear, you'll see him again shortly," she said, smirking as she stroked my cheek. "Besides, it's not like you're going anywhere else. With every trial you complete, I get stronger. And you, unfortunately, will get weaker. Eventually—"

She stopped, as, in that moment, I was able to break free from the cloud of darkness around my legs. My constant wriggling had paid off. I was able to kick her with all my force. I slammed my feet into her torso, which sent her flying.

This also released me from the rest of the cloud of darkness, which faded away and immediately dropped me to the ground. Without any hesitation, I dashed to the flashlight that was on the ground next to Kirsten's frozen body.

When the mistress finally got back on her feet, her cheeks burned with rage. She summoned a gust of darkness towards me.

I gazed at the flashlight in my hand, staring blanking at the seemingly encrypted message etched into it. Then I aimed the flashlight towards the darkness. I held my breath and flicked the switch on the flashlight.

The light beaming from the flashlight illuminated the entirety of the place I was in. I was defending myself with the light from the flashlight. Something about this flashlight seemed oddly familiar. It was as if I'd seen it before when I was a child.

I gradually made my way to her. Before I had a chance to burn her, though, she had whisked me to the next trial.

Just like during the last trial, she had somehow forced her way inside me. Instead of giving in this time, I was willing to fight.

It wasn't long until my gaze had fallen on the next victim—Liam. The moment I saw his face I knew. I couldn't bring myself to murder the man who had stood by me ever since I had joined the military and even that night when I'd first met him.

The mistress had made me kill innocent people. But not Liam. I couldn't bear the thought of sticking a gun to his forehead like I had the others. So instead I threw myself to the ground, refusing to do what she wanted.

"No. You can't make me," I screamed. *"You can't make me do it!"*

She seemed ever angrier than she normally was. She released herself from me. She faced me and reached her hand behind her. A knife appeared in her left hand as she slowly brought it from behind her back.

I aimed the torch at her. But before I could switch it on, she slapped it out of my hands and blasted a gust of darkness towards me that knocked me off my feet.

I was about to get back up, but I was forcefully pinned down. She pushed her foot into my back. With those heels she was wearing, the pain was unbearable.

I rolled over and grabbed her ankles in an attempt to drag her down. But as I did so, she threw the knife, aiming it at Liam's heart.

I gazed on in shock. A river of tears flowed down my face. "No!" I screamed as I ran toward his body.

The colour was slowly draining from his face. He looked deep into my eyes, and I looked deep into his.

His hand slowly extended toward my cheek. *Can he see me?* I wondered. And he could.

I placed my hand gently on his. All I could say was, "I'm sorry."

I turned my head towards the mistress. I was angry—no, not angry. I was furious. None of this was my fault. I had fallen into this trap long ago. It was then I finally realised I was nothing more than a puppet of the darkness. She never wanted to help me save my brother.

All she ever wanted was to toy with me. She lied to me and said everything would be back to normal, when all this time, she had used me to get what she wanted.

That's why I was getting weaker every time I completed one of the trials. But why she wanted me to do the things she'd made me do I didn't know. What I did know was that she would probably plan something horrible if she got any stronger.

I grabbed my torch and lunged at the mistress. Just as I wrapped my arms around her waist, she whisked us both back to the dark place.

Before I continued to fight her, I used my flashlight to burn off the darkness that kept Kirsten frozen. As soon as she dropped to the floor, I placed her arm around my shoulder and held her up by the waist, using the flashlight to defend us from the darkness.

While fighting off my light, the Mistress of Darkness must have seen that I still had strength and determination. I saw in her eyes that she was surprised I had something inside me that enabled me to break free from her control.

The light began to feel stronger. Although the burning of the darkness threatened to overwhelm me, I felt stronger than ever. For the first time in my life, I felt the strength of my will, and I was able to use the light to get back.

I was able to make the mistress's gust of darkness backfire on her. I pointed the flashlight, held Kirsten tightly, and ran. Just like magic, the light illuminated my path. And just like that, I was whisked back to reality, along with Kirsten—with the power of the light.

———◆◆>|◆<◆●———

Matthew was helping Harry go through the security cameras when, all the sudden, a bright light illuminated the room, and Kirsten and I jumped out of it.

The boys looked on in awe. Matthew kneeled down and wrapped his arms around me. All I could do was return the embrace.

Harry went over to Kirsten. Just as had happened with him and Matthew, she was regaining consciousness now that she was back from the place of darkness—only with a twist. She remembered certain experiences from being trapped in the mistress's dark place.

As soon as she saw me, she wrapped her arms around me tightly and began to tear up slightly. "Thank you," she said softly.

Matthew and Kirsten gave me a group hugged. Only Harry hung back.

Chapter 5

The Mission

Liam's Final Thoughts

After Liam received the knife through his heart, through his subconscious, the sensation of dying felt emotionally welcoming; all he could think about was his deceased daughter.

Liam also thought of his wife back in their apartment complex in New York and how she would feel when she found out that he was dead.

Liam's wife, Rita, had completely lost herself when they'd lost their only daughter. If it weren't for Liam's constant loyalty and love she would have given up on life a long time ago.

Rita hadn't wanted Liam to join the army, even though it paid well. They had gone through a tough money crisis after their daughter passed. But Rita never cared about the money. They would pull through no matter what—all because she loved Liam with all her heart. She had loved him ever since they were seniors flirting in high school.

Liam could only shed tears as he embraced the light. To his surprise, he was warmly welcomed by his daughter.

"Daddy!" she cried, her voice echoing sweetly from within the light.

Liam slowly got up and made his way up in the heavenly light. There she was, still beautiful as ever. *Just like her mother*, he thought as he burst into tears of joy. He embraced his daughter in his arms.

His face was drenched in tears and messy. He smiled fully for the first time in fifteen years. He finally got to see his little girl again.

◆━━◆━◆

It had been a whole week, and I hadn't left my apartment. All I ever did was lie on my bed and feel sorrow for the people the darkness had made me kill.

The fact that I had been used made me sick to my stomach.

Kirsten and Harry were getting debriefed by General Howard on our first mission together. We would be getting be shipped off to Afghanistan to eliminate four Taliban generals in Rharib Ail's Scasura.

Matthew didn't attend the debriefing, as he was worried about me. It was sweet of him to care about me. But I couldn't possibly feel sympathy for myself after what I had done.

While sitting at the edge of my bed, I heard a knock on my door. I couldn't bring myself to face anyone. It wasn't until I heard Matthew's voice on the other side of the door that I considered opening it.

At first I hesitated. Ever since I had been released from the Mistress of Darkness's clutches, I'd felt wrong. All I felt was depression slowly creeping in as the guilt overwhelmed my emotions.

I eventually got up and unlocked the door. I politely asked Matthew to come in as sat back down on the end of my bed.

I could see in Matthew's eyes that all he felt was remorse. Seeing me in such a state made his eyes water up. He closed the door and sat next to me. I told him what I had suffered through.

He gently wrapped his arm around me as I continued. And like the caring friend he is, he listened.

After I finished he let out a deep sigh. "We all do things we regret. And like you, we've all been used or taken advantage of. But as with everything that goes on in life, we must move on. My grandmother would always say that the mistakes we make in life are what make us a better person in the future."

I turned to face Matthew and looked deep into his emerald green eyes—eyes that any woman could get lost in. Like they always say, the eyes are the windows to the soul. What I saw was a kind, caring, and passionate man.

Tears dripped down my cheek. Matthew tucked a piece of my hair that had fallen down on my face behind my ear.

While gazing into each other's eyes, it seemed we both had the same sensation. We leaned in at the same time. As soon as our lips touched, an essence of beauty crept into my emotions. It was as if all the negativity was slowly fading away. Matthew and I embraced, holding each other closely. I gently caressed his hair, and he ran his fingers through mine. We leaned onto the bed in a tender loving moment.

Liam's Body Returns Home

After Liam's body was found, one of the sergeants insisted that his body be returned home.

The man pondered this mission endlessly, especially thinking back to how many good men and women they had lost, not long after they had gotten here.

The sergeant knew Afghanistan was a tough place. It was his fourth tour here. He had seen soldiers come and go. The state of the survivors was unbearable. Surviving through Afghanistan left its mark. Memories of the horrific tragedies they'd witnessed forever stayed with them. Not even the strongest individuals were immune to the effects of the horrifying tragedies.

Ever since the civilians of Afghanistan had started to gossip around their villages and the location of Rharib Ail's Scasura had gotten out to the soldiers, there had been constant Taliban attacks—everything from ambushes to sniper attacks.

General Howard's last tour to Afghanistan was the worst he'd ever seen. To this day, the memories haunted him. His reaction had caused his wife to leave him and his children to be scared of him.

When one the sergeants contacted him about Liam, the first thought in General Howard's mind was Liam's wife. He knew what Liam and his wife had gone through with their daughter. Now with Liam gone, his wife would be in a far more delicate state.

When the Chinook landed at the base, the remaining soldiers from Liam's squad loaded his body onto the helicopter. He was strapped in. Once the Chinook was refuelled and the pilot had had a rest break and something to eat, she returned and began the journey back home—with Liam's body in tow.

———————◆♦)◆(◆———————

Back in Washington at the base, General Howard was explaining to me and the others about the crucial and dangerous mission we had to fulfil in Afghanistan. Even though this was the first mission I would take on, I'd be leading the entire operation—along with Harry, who would accompany me on the mission.

Kirsten, being a fully qualified sniper, would be hidden nearby to support the squad and eliminate anyone who tried to get close to me.

Matthew would remain at the base on location, navigating the security monitors and finding the location of the four generals.

Rita Finds Out

The day Liam's wife was notified of his death, she emotionally broke down. One of the soldiers had gone to her place to deliver the bad news.

As soon as the soldier left, Rita closed the door. She broke down and collapsed to her knees. She cried with all her heart, as she felt it breaking all over again.

Rita's mind rushed back to that day her daughter had died. Now with Liam gone, she felt nothing but emptiness. The man she had fallen for in high school, the man who had stuck by her side, the man who had kept his word from his wedding vows was gone.

It wasn't long until Rita's phone began to ring. At first she couldn't bring herself to answer. Her face was drenched in tears and messy. Her vision was blurry because of the tears that filled her eyes.

She slowly got up from her knees and made her way to her mobile phone. It was Liam's mother, Rita's mother-in-law.

Rita hadn't gotten along with her family ever since her mother had passed away. Her siblings hadn't wanted her to inherit half of her mother's fortune.

But when she'd met Liam's family, she had instantly been welcomed. Liam's mother felt proud to have Rita as a daughter-in-law. Liam loved her and worshipped the ground she walked on. She clearly was the woman of his dreams.

Recently, Liam had started to work late because of an "unusual anomaly" that needed his attention. Liam normally never hid anything about his work from his wife. Most of the things he told her about were complex, so he never went into full detail.

Liam had mentioned Scarlet. But he hadn't told her about whatever the anomaly was related to her; all he'd said was that it was important and that it would remain classified.

Rita knew she'd probably meet Scarlet at Liam's funeral. She'd see for herself what this Scarlet was like.

Liam's Funeral

While waiting for things to settle down and while Liam's family planned his funeral, General Howard, was getting endless reports from the crew in Afghanistan. Many others had perished. He started to have regrets about the missions there. Since rumours of that hidden village had gotten out, the deaths had seemed endless.

Howard looked at his board. Pinned to it were pictures of Scarlet, Matthew, Kirsten, and Harry. "You four are our last hope," he said taking out his hip flask.

———◆◆◆◆———

I was training with the others. Today and tomorrow would be our last days of being home. By Saturday we'd be heading to Afghanistan.

Since that day in my room, Matthew and I had grown closer than ever. Even though I wasn't ready for a relationship, it was still nice to have him close.

Harry entered the gym where Matthew, Kirsten, and I were training and told us there was a special request for the four of us to carry Liam's coffin at his funeral tomorrow.

Kirsten demanded to look at the request order sheet before she replied, "Shouldn't members of Liam's family have that honour?" She gave the sheet of paper back to Harry.

"I agree with Kirsten. Why us?" I asked.

Harry was just as surprised as we were. He shrugged. "Orders came from General Howard himself."

———◆◆◆◆◆———

The next morning after we got breakfast, we went back to our apartments to get ready for Liam's funeral.

I went through my wardrobe, searching for an outfit to wear that was descent enough. I'm not your typical girlie girl, but I'm not a typical tomboy either. I always found something that looked good on me, and it never had to be super stylish or really cool and casual.

I picked a knee-length dress with a dark black rose in the middle over the chest.

I put it on and checked myself out in the mirror. Suddenly, my face in the mirror morphed, and the Mistress of Darkness's face was looking back at me.

I stumbled back, trying to get away from the mirror. I was determined not to let her get inside my head ever again.

But she could still torment me. Her whispering echoed in my ears as she blamed me for all the murders. But I knew it wasn't true—even though, if I told someone what had happened, they'd lock me up; they'd think I was crazy.

The only people I could trust were my friends. Sure they might not fully understand. They never would. Only I knew the truth, and that made me breathe easier.

———◆◆◆◆◆———

After we got dressed, we met up next to the car park. Rita and some of Liam's family had arrived. When I introduced myself to Rita, she went quiet all of a sudden, and then she slowly walked away. At first I was curious, but I brushed it off. She was probably still in mourning over Liam.

The car that carried the coffin arrived, along with two other cars. Kirsten, Matthew, Harry, General Howard, and I would go in on. Rita and Liam's parents and two siblings would go in the other.

After we had loaded the coffin into the car, we all got in and were taken to a cathedral. Kirsten and I were bewildered. "They must have saved an absolute bitching fortune to have Liam's funeral service here," Kirsten said, sounding both surprised and curious.

I agreed with her. A cathedral like this seemed rare. Like Kirsten had said, it must have cost Liam's family a fortune.

As Liam's family and friends took their seats inside the cathedral, Pastor Clements came outside to talk about the arrangements. General Howard was to be seated in his arranged seat. And we learned that Liam's younger brother, Edward, would be carrying Liam's coffin with us.

During the service, tears streamed down the faces of Liam's family. Rita never stopped crying, the tears were as endless as a rapid river. And her heart was like a delicate flower that broke over and over and over again.

I heard Pastor Clements say, "He shall be in our father's loving arms and in the embrace of his beloved lost daughter. It is the foul evil of war, the devil's plaything that caused this pain in our hearts."

It killed me that I only knew the truth about how Liam had died. And I could see her still, even though I had escaped. But she couldn't manipulate like before. As of now, all she could do was stand down and look on from a far. As of now, I would kill for her no more.

A Farewell from Home

After the service was over, the whispering echoes started again. I suddenly had an idea why the darkness was doing it. She had touched me, which meant we shared a link. Sure I had been able to break free from her bondage. But her presence was still there—haunting me, never leaving, goading me into finishing the trials.

When we got back to our apartments on base, I packed up my gear for tomorrow. My head started to throb, and the old flashbacks started to rush through my head like a flickering movie trailer.

But soon it stopped. I regained control. The pounding in my head disappeared. At first I questioned it. But I tried not think about it too much. I wasn't gonna let her play me ever again.

The next morning was an early one. After the Chinooks had arrived and refuelled, General Howard ordered myself and my team to the first Chinook. The army infantry team was ordered to go on the second Chinook.

Before Matthew could strap himself in, he did one final check through his rucksack for the predator drone he would be bringing along. When he finally found it in the side pocket of his rucksack, the relief on his face made Kirsten giggle.

"Feeling sentimental, Poindexter." She laughed.

Matthew just looked at her sarcastically. "Ha ha. What a classic Kirsty."

Kirsten punched him on his arm.

That was one thing about Kirsten. She never liked being called by any nicknames. Even though we were friends and she could trust us, Kirsten still held some of the painful memories of her pig-head father close. Not only did nicknames hurt her feelings, they shamefully reminded her of the cruel, harsh life she'd lived when she was a child.

Just after Matthew apologised, General Howard got on board.

The Chinook's doors closed; it was the last day I'd see home for awhile.

<hr />

In Afghanistan, the situation was only getting tenser by the minute.

Corporal Meadows and Sergeant Barnes had just finished escorting the British infantry unit back to base.

"Dude, I'm not sure things are getting better out there. It's a right shithole," Barnes said, pointing out that they'd been dodging endless bullets.

"Thanks, Barnes. It's not like I haven't noticed."

Meadows was interrupted when a grenade, hurled by the Taliban, landed at their feet. If it wasn't for Barnes's quick thinking, it may well have been the end for them both. He grabbed Meadows by his arm and dragged him inside the base. Just before the gates closed, the grenade exploded behind them, burning Corporal Meadows's right arm.

"Thanks, bud," Meadows said as he patted Barnes on the back.

"No problem, mate," Barnes replied in his British accent.

An Unfortunate Landing

After several hours of flying and endless radio reports from the squad already in Afghanistan, my stomach was on edge. All sorts of things were happening in Afghanistan. I'd never picture myself going to a place like this.

Kirsten could tell I was uneasy. She gently wrapped her arm around my shoulder and told me I'd be fine. That was easy for her to say, since she's been there before.

To be honest, though, they were all scared. Matthew wasn't so much scared as he was worried, since he wouldn't be the one away from the base.

Harry clearly felt tense the entire journey, clenching his fists together. He may have been a veteran, but that didn't mean he wasn't scared. Everything he had heard about the recent happenings in Afghanistan made him doubt their chances of survival.

Kirsten tried to remain as confident as she could, and I appreciated it. She would potentially be at risk, being mine and Harry's personal backup. Even though she'd be hidden, there was a possibility she would be compromised. I knew this terrified her, since that had never happened to her before.

After several hours of flying, we'd made it to the Afghan border. That was when until things started to take a turn for the worse.

The Taliban began firing missiles from their RPGs at the Chinooks. The pilot and the co-pilot tried to manoeuvre the Chinook to dodge the incoming missiles. But one missile hit the back, blowing the back end of the helicopter completely off.

The force from the explosion was massive. We all hung on for dear life. My hands lost their grip and I stumbled onto the platform. Luckily, I was able to get another grip and held on as my legs were flying in the air. The pilot began to lose control of the Chinook.

Harry went to grab my hand, but I caught a glimpse of another missile coming towards us. I let go and landed on my ankle, hearing a crunch from the force of the drop.

Luckily, the pilot managed to rotate the Chinook, and the missile narrowly missed us.

"Grab the parachutes and bail out!" General Howard shouted.

Everyone except the pilot and co-pilot grabbed a parachute. As soon as we had gotten them on, we jumped.

———◆◆✦◆◆———

The co-pilot turned and saw one last parachute. Without any hesitation, he took off his headset and bolted to the parachute. Throwing it on, he jumped. The pilot was angry that her co-pilot would abandon her. It wasn't long before the final missile hit, and the Chinook burst into flames.

Straight to Business

After the unfortunate landing, I was immediately seen to by one of the medics for my ankle, which wasn't broken. Luckily it was only a minor sprain and would heal up in a couple of weeks. The medic prescribed me some painkillers.

———◆◆✦◆◆———

Meanwhile, General Howard met up with Captain Abernathy, Corporal Meadows, and Sergeant Barnes.

Captain Abernathy was a lot like General Howard. He, too, had that hard-ass attitude and the stale taste of whiskey on his breath. The look in his eyes when he saw the squad that would be tasked to eliminate the four Taliban generals said it all. "The way things are going out there, I'm not betting on their safe return," he said.

———◆◆✦◆◆———

While General Howard was still talking to Captain Abernathy, Sergeant Barnes noticed Kirsten. He hadn't seen he since her last tour in Afghanistan. He and Corporal Meadows carried out a heavy duffel bag that contained Kirsten's personal sniper rifle.

They both dropped the bag down beside her. Kirsten was on their case immediately. "Hey!" she snapped. "Watch it. That's my prized beauty in there." She was concerned about her precious, which she'd dubbed "Sandy."

Ever since Kirsten had become a combat marine, she'd dreamed she would eventually hold a sniper rifle in her hands. Every time she picked up old Sandy, she'd say, "It feels like an organism in my hands."

"You talking to that gun again?" Barnes said in his cheeky manner.

Kirsten started to joke around with Barnes.

It was then that Corporal Meadows recognised Harry. He still looked like the same man who he'd served with in the US Navy—even after the incident with his close friend that had caused Harry to isolate himself.

"Hey, Armanton!" Meadows called. "How's things going with the fiancée?"

He didn't know that Harry hadn't spoke to his fiancée since the incident with his friend—it had broken him, stripping him of all emotions.

"I don't know." Harry's tone was distant. "We haven't spoken since that day." He was forbidden to be near his wife-to-be until he received proper psychiatric help. And he had refused help. He still blamed himself for what had happened to his friend.

For Luck

This morning, waking up in Afghanistan felt like waking up in a bad dream. In my mind, I was thinking through what I was gonna face out there.

After General Howard and Captain Abernathy gave me the debriefing, I studied the details we had on the four Taliban generals and the endless reports on Rharib Ail's Scasura.

Matthew came into the tent I was in. He was about to set up his monitors. "Kirsten's heading out to her sniping position, and the transport for you and Harry is arriving in half an hour," Matthew said. Then he looked at me, looking rather concerned.

Matthew stood beside me with his hand on my shoulder. "You okay?" he asked gently.

I was about to turn my head towards him, but my eyes were drawn to the endless reports. "To be honest, Matthew, I'm terrified."

Matthew knew everyone else was scared too. "Scarlet, look at me."

I slowly got up and faced him.

He put his hands on my cheeks. "After everything you've been through, you can get through this. I … we all believe in you."

I looked into his eyes. Then we leaned towards each other and shared our second kiss.

We pulled back and looked into each other's eyes again. Matthew caressed my cheek.

"For luck," I said gently.

We smiled at each other, and then I grabbed my gear and headed out.

Matthew's heart was beating rapidly as he watched me get into the truck with Harry.

Sniper's Nest

While Harry and Scarlet were being secretly transported to the hidden village, Kirsten was transported to her sniper's nest on top of a steep hill that required a lot of climbing.

After the climb, Kirsten picked out her position. She crawled down to the point she had chosen and surveyed the surroundings through her scope, looking over Rharib Ail' Scasura.

She had an uneasy feeling about the entire village. The entire surrounding area seemed more like a base camp for the Taliban than a village.

<hr />

Matthew and I surveyed the area we were about to enter. I felt sickened when I saw how the women were treated forcefully. I watched a woman being grabbed by the arms and dragged inside one of the buildings.

"Are they taking them where I think they're taking them?" I said.

Harry placed his hand on my shoulder and nodded sternly.

I reached into my rucksack and took out a small device of Matthew's called a drone camera. I brought it online and used my headset to get in contact with Matthew.

"Matthew, switch to prototype drone B5-92 omega 1," I said.

Matthew quickly brought the prototype online. I envisioned him using the joystick in front of his monitors to lift the drone from my hand. "All right, it's online," Matthew said when the camera on the drone had been activated.

I ordered Matthew to use the drone to see what was inside the building where the soldiers had taken the young women.

"Guys, you've gotta move. Five Taliban soldiers are coming your way," Kirsten said over the coms. She had been scanned the area with her scope and had spotted the squad.

Harry and I needed to quickly move to a safe position. But first, Harry quickly planted landmines and concealed them under the sand.

I turned and looked at Harry and told him to hurry up. He told me to go on ahead, and he went another direction.

"Kirsten, hold your fire," Harry ordered.

At first, I was worried. But I continued on, climbing inside the vent of the building that Matthew's drone camera had gone into.

As I crawled through the vent, Harry hid under a truck. He gave the order to Kirsten to open fire on the five Taliban soldiers. She delivered every shot, raising her kill count by five.

Through the Vents

As I crawled through vents, echoes of Arabic banter and laughter floated to my ears. I peeked through the air ducts. The sights I saw were utterly revolting. For the most part, I covered my eyes.

I knew the women had no say in these parts of the country. And mostly they would obey their religious rights, which never really made sense to me.

I continued on through the vents. Harry came up with the idea to rig the place to blow. He explained an idea to get the civilians out of here after we eliminated the generals.

I took some C-4 from my backpack and planted the explosives outside next to the air ducts.

Once I was finished, I turned my headset back on. Matthew and Kirsten were bantering as they surveyed the area. Kirsten continued to take out the squads that were probably coming to the village for R&R.

I noticed the vent began to feel unstable. While I was to trying to find a suitable place to get out of the vent, Kirsten and Matthew started talking about me. Before Kirsten got to the bit about the kiss, I interrupted, startling the both of them, especially Kirsten.

"How are things looking in there, Scar?" Matthew sounded rather concerned.

I was taken aback by the nickname—since nobody had called me Scar before.

Suddenly, the vent broke apart below me, and I fell to the ground, attracting the attention of every Taliban in and around the room, including the generals.

One of the Generals grabbed me by the neck and started stroking my cheeks. When Harry rushed in, the general let go of me. I grabbed my pistol from its holster and fired multiple shots into the general's chest. Meanwhile, Harry took down the three remaining generals with his assault rifle.

After we took down the generals, Kirsten reported that the entire town was swarming with Taliban soldiers. She fired shot after shot from her sniper rifle.

Unfortunately for Kirsten, a group of Taliban was heading her way. But she was too focused on the village to notice, as there were too many of them.

Back in the building, Harry and I were fighting our way out. But too many assailants were swarming into the building. We didn't stand a chance.

They were able to grab us and knock us out.

Sniper Captured

Kirsten tried to get a hold of Scarlet and Harry, but they had gone dark. Maybe Matthew would have some valuable information.

What she didn't realise was that Matthew's drone camera had been destroyed in the gunfire, so he was blind.

Suddenly, his voice came over the coms. "Kirsten, you've gotta retreat. Kirsten?! Kirsten, respond. You've gotta retreat."

Before Kirsten could respond, she noticed a shadow above her. She swiftly turned to see a Taliban soldier reaching to grab her by the waist. But before he could even get one finger onto her, Kirsten quickly jumped to her feet, twirled around, as she manoeuvred behind the soldier, and whacked him on the back of his head with Sandy. Then shot him at point-blank range.

"You just got 3.60 no scoped, bitch," Kirsten said looking down at the dead Taliban soldier on the ground.

While she was busy gloating, another soldier took her off guard. He grabbed her by the waist, throwing both of them off her sandy perch atop the steep and stony mountain. Kirsten and the Taliban soldier fought over who would get the safest landing, until, unfortunately for him, Kirsten kicked the soldier with all her force. He landed head first into the hot, rocky mountainside.

Kirsten kept tumbling. She tried to use her emergency parachute, realising quickly that it was still on the mountaintop. So she braced herself for a rough, painful landing.

Kirsten landed on her side. She felt like she'd broken a few ribs. She couldn't even attempt to move, as she was in agony.

The remaining Taliban soldiers who'd found Kirsten's location had confiscated Sandy. Kirsten continued to fight, kicking any soldier who approached her in the groin. Whenever she hit one, he'd let out a hilarious Arabic moan. This made Kirsten snicker—until one of the soldiers used Sandy to knock her out.

Then he scooped her up and carried her to the village.

Chapter 6

Betrayal

Prisoners of the Taliban

Harry and I were both locked up in some sort of boiler room. We were chained up like animals. Harry seemed pretty calm as he dangled the chain on his shackles. "Just wait for the fucking torture," he said.

"Not like this isn't torture enough" I thought to myself with my head against the wall. Meanwhile, I was terrified. You hear about stuff like this in TV documentaries or movies. But experiencing it yourself was entirely different. This felt more like one bad dream in the middle of another bad dream.

It wasn't long until we heard Kirsten kicking and cursing at the soldiers as they dragged her in here and chained her up. Harry stared daggers at the Taliban. He swung the chain of his shackles and pounced on one of the soldiers, threatening to strangle him to death if they didn't let us go.

The others pointed their AK-47s at him. He tightened the chain around the soldier's throat. Then one of the soldiers pinned Harry to the wall, and bashed his face into it. Next—I could hardly bare to watch—they pinned Harry to the wall, and one soldier took out his machete and sliced Harry's right hand clean off.

Harry's scream was endless. He knelt on the floor clutching his right arm, which was bleeding profusely. Just before the soldiers left, one of them had soccer kicked Harry in the stomach, which made him wince even more.

"I can't tell which one of you looks worse," Kirsten said, doing her best to be her sarcastic self.

Harry responded with, "Glad to see you're still a sarcastic bitch." He gradually sat up straight, still clenching his right arm tightly. He didn't even bother to look at his missing hand.

"Has this ever happened to you before?" I asked cautiously. "I mean, have you been caught?"

Kirsten seemed pleased to talk, since it would keep her mind busy and off the pain she was in. "In all my years of being a marine sniper, I've never been captured," she said, adding, "Well not like this."

Harry spoke up. "Back in the day when Afghanistan wasn't this bad of a threat. But ever since the rumours about this village started up, the whole place is like one big shit storm."

Bring the American Females

I wasn't sure how long we'd been locked up, when a group of Taliban soldiers came into the room, unchained Kirsten and I, and dragged us out to God knows where. Kirsten kicked and cursed at the soldiers. They dragged us to some sort of intimidation room, where they sat us down and chained us each to a chair.

They started with me, questioning me about who I was and who I worked for.

I heard Kirsten whisper, "Don't tell them anything, Scar."

One of the soldiers placed the blade of his machete against Kirsten's neck.

Kirsten spat in his face, which angered the soldier beyond belief.

Since I wasn't giving them any information, they decided to try a new tactic. A soldier dragged Kirsten by her hair and held her up in front of me. "Maybe you will loosen your tongue, if we inflict suffering on your comrade," snarled the second in command.

He took out his dagger, placed it against my cheek, and gently slit it open, leaving a bloody gash. He then leaned in close. As he looked me in the eye, he pushed his fingers onto my bleeding cheek.

Then he moved on to Kirsten.

The more they made Kirsten suffer, the greater was my urge to tell them everything. But I knew I couldn't. And Kirsten knew too. She kept telling me not to.

At one point, the second in command grew impatient. He readied his dagger and grabbed Kirsten by the neck. Her face was completely beat up. Her left eye was black and blue and swollen, and she barely could open it.

The second in command looked at me, smirking. Tears filled my eyes. I watched in sheer horror as he lifted his blade and spoke a sacred Arabic saying that I couldn't even understand. Moving the blade closer and closer to Kirsten's face, he turned to me again. But I still refused to talk. He stabbed Kirsten right in her left eye.

Her constant screaming was too much to bear. But I couldn't break—no matter how painful it was to hear. I knew Kirsten would agree, which made me feel less guilty.

General Howard's True Colours

General Howard had heard what was going on from Corporal Meadows. His expression changed. It was time to take matters into his own hands. He commanded Captain Abernathy to gather the remaining infantry troops and march onward to Matthew's surveillance tent.

Matthew was in a complete panic. The communications weren't responsive, and his prototype drone camera had been destroyed in the firefight. He was completely blind to what was happening.

That was until, suddenly, Scarlet's headset was activated. Before Matthew could react, General Howard came up behind him and pushed him roughly off his chair. As Matthew fell to the floor.

General Howard took control of the radio. He'd had a lot of experience with the Arabic language and was mostly fluently.

Matthew, who had been stunned by the general's surprise blow, came back to himself. But before he could get up, Corporal Meadows and Sergeant Barnes grabbed him by the arms.

After General Howard was done speaking, he put the microphone down and slowly walked towards Matthew. "Don't worry," he said, a bit suspiciously. He added, as if hiding his suspicious behaviour with bluntness,

"I've arranged some sort of agreement." Then he ordered Meadows and Barnes to let go of Matthew.

Matthew grabbed General Howard's arm. "What arrangement?" he demanded.

General Howard shook his arm free and began to lie to Matthew. The truth was all of them—Scarlet, Harry, and Kirsten (especially Scarlet)—were now lost causes.

Back at the village, soldiers swarmed into the boiler room, where Kirsten and I had been returned after the failed interrogation. They grabbed Harry, Kirsten, and me roughly and took us to a transport truck. They sat us on the floor of the truck, while the soldiers who would be accompanying us sat on benches, keeping an eye on us.

Kirsten kept cursing and spitting in their faces. Even with her missing eye and the agonising pain she was in, she still had her fiery attitude that kept her strong. The spitting cost her a few more beatings, but she never flinched.

Harry tried to keep it together. The pain from his missing hand made him sick to his stomach. But he never showed weakness. Both him and Kirsten stayed strong for me.

After an hour-long drive, they dragged us out and kicked us to the ground right in front of General Howard, who, surprisingly, didn't seem very welcoming.

"Scar!" Matthew shouted as he made his way to us.

But he was stopped by Captain Abernathy, who held him back as he struggled to get free.

The second in command—ya know, Kirsten's torturer—greeted General Howard like old friends as he handed him a weekly supply of munitions and sold us to the Taliban.

"Do to them as you wish, General. They are my gift to you." Before he left, he added with a sly smirk, "Just make sure she suffers." He pointed at me.

"She will know suffering beyond her darkest imaginings," the second in command replied as he flicked away his cigar. He walked closer to me. "I have plans for you, American."

Parwan Detention Facility

We all knew General Howard had been suspicious of me from the start. But seeing him greet this Taliban general like they were old friends was too much.

I could tell that Harry saw red and that he wanted to kill General Howard right here and now. He struggled to get loose from his captor.

After General Howard shook his hand, the second in command grabbed me by the back of my neck.

As I struggled to get loose from his grip, I caught a glimpse of Matthew, who was being held back by Meadows and Abernathy. Seeing this, I was utterly distraught.

***

After Kirsten, Harry, and I were put back in the trucks, General Howard turned to Matthew and looked deeply into his eyes. "It's for the best." He paused, patted Matthew's shoulder, and added in a whisper, "Don't you think."

***

Back in the truck, our captors strapped chains around our necks, like we were animals.

"I can't believe General Howard sold us out," Harry said under his breath. I could feel his rage over General Howard's betrayal.

"How could he sell us out like that?" I asked. I tried to keep my mind from thinking about what was gonna happen to us.

Kirsten remained silent, which wasn't like her at all. She buried her face into her hands and rocked slowly backwards and forwards. I moved towards her and gently wrapped my arm around her.

Kirsten smirked a little. She gently kissed my forehead and rested her head on my shoulder as she held my hand tightly.

As much as I was terrified about what was gonna happen to us, I felt an urge to be strong for my friends. They had been strong for me. This was the worst shape I'd ever seen them in, especially Kirsten.

A Sight Never to Be Forgotten

We had been driving for about four hours when the truck came to a stop. Taliban soldiers opened the back of the truck and grabbed our chains to drag us out like wild dogs. We all fought to adjust to the blinding sunlight.

My eyes were the first to adjust and the sight that appeared before me was an image I would certainly never forget.

Parwan detention facility resembled some sort of concentration camp. It was something like the camps the Nazis kept Jews and other captives in during World War II. Knowing this was what the Taliban was doing to people made me sick to my stomach. It was like history was rewriting itself.

They dragged us across to a nearby bunker past pens full of people calling out for freedom. Mothers tried to calm their sick, crying children. My eyes filled with tears. I saw what looked like a five-year-old girl with large spots covering her face and bruises all over her arms and legs. All you could see was black and blue.

The second in command ordered the soldiers to strap us to three individual chairs. They branded us with a branding iron, marking us with an Arabic symbol on our right legs to claim ownership. It was a treasonous mark, and the process was agonisingly painful. We winced in pain.

For once, I wished for the Mistress of Darkness to show herself. Maybe she could stop the Taliban. But she was nowhere. I started to wonder, Did I really drive her away? Then I recalled that she had still been around on the day of Liam's funeral. She had stood in front of me, just watching me.

After they branded us, one of the soldiers tried to get really personal with Kirsten. She kicked him in the crotch and blurted out, "If you're not a fine-looking woman with a fine-looking booty, you can get lost."

The soldier didn't seem pleased. He rushed towards her with his machete drawn and pressed it to her throat.

Then he turned and spotted me. But before he could come anywhere near me, the second in command stopped him. "No!" he snapped. "I have plans for this one." He glanced at me. "Why don't you take these two where the dishonourable traitors are held."

After he gave that order, the soldiers dragged Kirsten and Harry away.

When they were gone, he turned to me. Placing his hands on the arms of the chair, he looked deep into my eyes. "Let's see if we can break you, perfect one." He patted my cheek and then gently kissed it.

I spat in his eye.

He wiped his eye and looked at his fingers with the spit. Then he balled his hand into a fist and punched me in the face, knocking me out.

Matthew and Barnes's Rebellion

Matthew couldn't believe he had witnessed his friends being taken away, thanks to General Howard. He knew he had to find a way to rescue them. He scoured his security monitors for any clues or signs of where they might be. But when nothing turned up no matter where he looked, he got more and more frustrated.

As his frustration built, his heart began to ache. He thought of Scarlet and what the Taliban might be doing to her. And he thought about the darkness that haunted Scarlet and what might happen if the Taliban started to take advantage of her.

When Barnes came into the tent, Matthew didn't hesitate. He launched himself towards Barnes, the anger filling him. He grabbed Barnes by the front of his uniform threw several punches Barnes's way.

While deflecting Matthew's punches, Barnes tried to explain himself— to defend himself. At first, Matthew was having none of it. After all, Barnes had restrained him along with Corporal Meadows while General Howard had spoken to the Taliban's second in command.

Barnes was able to deflect Matthew's attacks. Eventually, though, Matthew was able to pin Barnes to the floor. Squeezing his wrists tightly, he pulled out his trench knife and placed it against Barnes's neck.

But when Barnes explained himself, Matthew's frown began to slowly disappear. It soon returned, and Matthew blurted out that Barnes was probably lying.

It wasn't the first time Barnes had been called a liar, even though he'd never been the lying type. Nevertheless, everyone he'd ever come into contact with (excluding his parents)—his ex-girlfriend, his college friends, his high school friends, and even his army buddies—had lobbed this accusation at him at one point or another. But they never meant anything serious, since Barnes was never one to be taken seriously.

After Barnes eventually convinced Matthew that he was telling the truth, the two of them agreed they have had to come up with a plan to rescue Scarlet, Harry, and Kirsten.

Matthew got out all the marked maps, showing known locations along the entire Afghan border. He searched through all the location data on his tablet-shaped computer. Barnes recommended rallying some of the other infantry teams, since some weren't led by General Howard. He also mentioned the AI, but it was programmed to follow orders from the higher-ups. Barnes suggested that Matthew could reprogram HILARY.

Matthew quickly replied with a no. Sure, he was great with computer technology. But reprogramming an AI was too complicated even for him.

Rebellion Side

Barnes took control of the infantry grunts who didn't follow General Howard's orders and had begun to view General Howard and Captain Abernathy's side as an enemy threat. The pair took control of one side of the base, and Matthew and Barnes's Rebellion took over the other side of the base.

Barnes felt a bit conflicted at first, as Meadows had taken General Howard's side. He and Meadows had been partnered here in Afghanistan, and Meadows had saved Barnes's life more times than he could possibly remember.

Matthew, the brains of the operation, was conducting a plan. He had searched the mapping data countless times.

Barnes had some of the combat engineers who had sided with them work on some special essentials for storming into Taliban territory.

Matthew was beating himself up for letting this happen. He swore to get his friends out of Taliban captivity.

Meanwhile, Barnes was holding off the armoury. It was located on the rebellion side of the base, which forced General Howard's side to try and take it by force. It was a difficult battle, but the rebels managed to hold onto the armoury, with only a minimum of casualties.

Perfect One

By the time I woke up, a few hours had passed since I had been knocked unconscious. I found myself in a different room. It seemed shadowed by darkness, and the air was moist, as if water had flooded the room and had only recently been drained out.

I lifted myself up, feeling my cheek where the cut had been made gingerly. My right eye was swollen and still partly closed.

I felt completely disgusted and lost. That the Taliban was keeping me here and had dubbed me "Perfect One" made sick to my stomach. I didn't want to know what they had planned for me.

But one thing I did know was that the Mistress of Darkness was watching me. I goaded her, hoping to get her to come to me. Now I knew the woman wasn't stupid. She knew I hated her with a passion because of what she had made me do. But this was my only option.

She came forward from the shadows and knelt me back down, kneeling down next to me. The light from the small window shined on my face, and the mistress risked the sheer pain to place her hand on my cheek.

"What have they done to you?" She spoke with remorse.

I never thought of her remorse as a sign of reformation or any hint of her changing her ways. The moment left me cautious. The mysterious woman had haunted me ever since I was ten years old. She'd put me through a series of psychotic episodes, leaving me in a constant state of anxiety. To actually see remorse on her face stunned me completely.

But before the Mistress of Darkness could make a decision about whether she was gonna help me, two Taliban soldiers stormed in with sly looks on their faces. They unchained me from the wall and grabbed me by my arms tightly so I couldn't get free.

Even as I was being dragged, I caught a glimpse of her staring daggers at me—or the soldiers. Either way, she seemed determined to do something. She faded into a cloud of darkness and followed like a predator stalking its prey.

Darkness versus Taliban

Because I was constantly struggling to get free, the two soldiers chained my arms and legs together and placed a blindfold over my eyes. This put me in a state of panic. My hands and knees trembled uncontrollably.

Meanwhile, the Mistress of Darkness continued to follow. The small oil lamps that lit the place began to flicker, and the room began to feel as cold as Antarctica.

The soldiers put me on a wooden table and strapped my wrists and ankles tightly so I couldn't get free.

They kept looking around. They knew something was up. Their skin shivered from the drafts of cold piercing their skin. One couldn't feel his fingers and toes, as they had gone completely numb from the sheer cold. The others ignored the painful cold, even as the temperature dropped.

The second in command pulled out a large syringe loaded with an experimental serum. "Years of development in Russia, months of testing in North Korea, and here it is—the famous and deadliest truth serum ever known to humankind. Even the strongest man is weak with it. Now let's see that pretty mouth of yours spill your guts." He pointed the needle at my neck.

Luckily for me, the Mistress of Darkness appeared in her human form. Her right hand shifted into a blade. She stabbed the second in command through his back, plunging the blade straight into his heart.

A look of sheer shock crossed his face as the colour drained from if. The others were in pure shock. They pointed their weapons into every corner of the room. But they couldn't see anything except themselves and me.

One of them grabbed me by my hair. He yanked my head back and forth and spoke angry words. But as they were in Arabic, I couldn't understand a word he said.

The Mistress of Darkness's blade-like arm impaled the soldier. She drove the blade into his chest and pulled him closer as he took his last breaths. "You may think you're something special. But really, you're nothing but savage gutter rats." Her sinister cold words echoed around the room.

To the soldiers, it sounded like the murmurings of a ghostly presence. Spooked, they fired their weapons, trying to goad the mysterious spirit presence.

To their shock, the Mistress of Darkness struck them like an assassin. She slashed and stabbed, showing no hint of mercy as she watched them bleed to death.

After gloating, she set me free, cutting my restraints off. I rubbed my wrists. The rope had burned my skin. I quickly got myself together and grabbed one of the AK-47s and the rounds from the other AKs on the floor.

"This is not a truce." I turned and faced her, staring into her eyes.

"Looks like we're even, aren't we," she replied with a smug smile on her face.

I continued to stare daggers at her; I didn't plan to show her any mercy.

Gear Up

Several hours of searching through the database archives on various locations on the Afghan border finally turned up a place called the Parwan detention facility. The facility had been built by the United States during the Bush administration but had since been taken over by the Taliban. Matthew had a good gut feeling that was where Scarlet, Kirsten, and Harry had been taken.

He immediately informed Barnes, who was preparing along with the other rebel. "Barnes! I know where the Taliban might have taken them," he exclaimed. He was carrying his portable tablet device.

"Parwan?" Barnes replied. "I've never heard of that before." He sounded rather confused. Most of Afghanistan had never been fully explored and further afield was all Taliban territory.

Barnes suggested that this rescue mission was a suicide attempt. The detention facility was far into Taliban territory. Matthew wasn't daft; he knew it was gonna be risky. But his friends meant the world to him.

Barnes was indecisive. Sure he wanted to rescue the trio. But the idea of going deep into unexplored Taliban territory made his stomach turn. Truthfully, he was petrified. Hell, he'd been more or less petrified ever since he'd first been stationed in Afghanistan. He was conscious of the many things here that would negatively affect his chance of survival.

Even though, this was the place where he'd lost his older sister. She'd been a recon marine medic stationed at this exact same base, back in the day before the rumours of the infamous mysterious village Rharib Ail's Scasura became to be a concern.

Barnes sighed deeply and arranged a plan to blow up the village, as well as the concentration camp. "That'll teach the Taliban we mean business."

After hearing Barnes's plan, Matthew decided to split the team into two groups. He and Barnes would each be in charge of a group. Barnes and his group would travel to Parwan facility and rescue Scarlet, Kirsten, and Harry, seeing how Barnes was capable of carrying out full assault operations.

Rescue Mission

The rebels were suited up, and their weapons were loaded. Matthew loaded himself up with full body armour, explosives, and a 9mm pistol. He also brought along his portable tablet device.

Barnes was fully equipped as well. He wore body armour and carried with him explosives and a 5.56 assault carbine standard service rifle, along with a standard trench shotgun for close-quarters combat and a Glock 19 for emergencies.

It was night-time, and Barnes and his squad were about to head out. Once they were geared up and fully loaded, they would set off for the Parwan detention facility.

Matthew caught up with him. "Bring them back safe." Matthew sounded concerned. As they had discussed, this rescue operation was likely a suicide mission.

Barnes nodded and smiled slightly. Then he climbed aboard the armoured Humvee and took point on the mounted machine gun.

Traveling at night was, in some ways, a huge risk. They had opted for night travel to keep the Taliban unalarmed. Still, there were other dangers and terrible tragedies they might face along the way to the concentration camp. Knowing this, they were a bit shaken. Most of the young men who were stationed in Afghanistan were grunts or newly experienced combat engineers who had never been thrown deep into battle.

The soldiers in the back of the trucks held their hands tightly together, breathing in and out slowly to calm their nerves and keep from trembling.

Their journey was, in deed, rough. They faced constant Taliban attacks and ambushes. Still, only a few of the men didn't make it. The casualties were a result of multiple bullet wounds sustained by the second group in the third Humvee behind Barnes's Humvee.

Finally, those among the squad who had survived the constant attacks arrived at the concentration camp. Barnes gathered his team altogether so they could arrange the plan of attack.

"Lasker, Dermott, you will take control of the mounted machine gun, providing us cover from enemy fire."

The two soldiers nodded in response.

"Markus, McDonnell, you will take charge of the explosives. Your mission will be to breach the main gate and any barricaded doors.

"The rest of us will give cover fire to Markus and McDonnell while they plant explosives and use the Humvees for cover."

When everyone in Barnes's squad had nodded in approval, Barnes pulled out his assault carbine rifle and moved behind one of the Humvees. From there, he gave a hand signal to Markus and McDonnell to set the explosives charges on the main gate.

The pair had successfully planted the charges and were making their way back to the Humvee when, like an eagle, one of the Taliban watch guards caught sight of them. Without warning he began shooting. Markus fell dead. McDonnell froze in place. When the guard started shooting again, McDonnell dove and grabbed the detonator from Markus's corpse and ran back toward the Humvees.

Just as he was about to reach Barnes, one of the guard's bullets struck him in his knee. He was forced to the ground, and the fear of dying slowly crept over him. He thought about his family back in Washington.

Barnes commanded one of the snipers to fire at the guard. He commanded the others to charge, at which point he would activate the detonator.

No sooner had the Taliban guard been dealt with than a guard on the other side of the post was alerted to their presence. It wouldn't be long before the rest of the guards were too.

Barnes carried McDonnell to safety and then took the detonator in his right hand. "Ready, steady, go," Barnes said.

He looked down to the main gate and activated the detonator. He clenched his eyes shut as the gate blew in a blinding burst of flames that burned with the heat of the sun.

When the explosion died down, Barnes commanded the Humvee drivers to storm in and eliminate any resistance that would outnumber the squad. The others, along with Barnes, stayed behind the Humvees for cover.

While fighting through the camp, Barnes spotted Kirsten and Harry in a pen where they were being held. He sent them assistance in the form of two grunts, who made their way to the pen, shooting at any Taliban soldier nearby. He followed closely behind.

Kirsten and Harry kept their heads covered as the shooting continued. When she spotted Barnes at the pen's gate, she beamed a smile of relief. She grabbed Harry's arm and hurled it over her shoulder. "We're getting out of here!" she said confidently.

Harry was delirious from massive blood loss. He tried to pull himself together, but the sensation of being conscious was making him sick and dizzy. He could hardly stand. His legs felt like jelly. His inability to walk made the escape even more difficult for Kirsten, who did most of the effort to keep both of them going.

The two grunts covered Barnes as he tried to destroy the lock. He pulled a grenade from his belt, pulled the pin, and placed the grenade on top of the lock. Moving back quickly back, he shouted at the top of his lungs, "*Stand back!*"

The two grunts covering Barnes moved back. Kirsten and Harry stood still at the back of the pen.

When the grenade exploded, the lock broke and disconnected from the gate, and the gate was bent from the force of the explosion. Barnes charged the gate and kicked it down, collapsing it inward.

Kirsten and Harry hurried to Barnes, who asked where Scarlet was. Kirsten said that Scarlet had been taken into the bunker. Barnes wasted no time in getting in there.

He called upon the two grunts to get Kirsten and Harry into the Humvee, while he carried on. Many of the squad had perished; only a small number of them had made it through thus far. Five of them went along with Barnes to infiltrate the bunker, and the remaining six rescued the poor innocents who were trapped in the other pens.

In the bunker, I was fighting off Taliban guards so I could make my escape from this horrible place. Even though I was using the Mistress of

Darkness to help me, I kept hearing what she had said to me about us being even in the back of my head. And it made me feel sick to my stomach. I would never consider us even after what she'd made me do.

Suddenly it occurred to me that I could hear a lot of gunfire outside. I paused for moment. Could it be a rescue team? I wasted no time and bolted out of there.

<hr/>

Barnes and his companions eliminated every Taliban soldier in the entrance inside the bunker. He commanded his five companions to set multiple charges around every corner of the bunker. While they split up, Barnes continued onward. It wasn't long before he reached a stone door that was controlled by a motion pad.

Barnes placed his right hand gently onto the motion pad. By luck, the pad turned green, and the stone door slid open to the left.

On the other side—putting an AK-47 in Barnes's face—was Scarlet.

<hr/>

I felt relieved when I saw Barnes. I asked him about this rescue, and he responded that it was all Matthew's idea. My heart skipped a beat. I knew Matthew would never abandon me, Kirsten, and Harry.

As soon as Kirsten and Harry came into my mind, I asked about them. Barnes reassured me. He placed his hand on my shoulder and told me that he had broken them out of the pen, and they were safely in one of the Humvees.

Back at the entrance, we met with Barnes's squad. Only four of the grunts he'd assigned to set the explosives returned. The fifth had been ambushed and shot multiple times.

I was stunned. The place looked like a burnt-out ruin. Fires littered the area. The guard posts, the pens, and the Taliban's tent barracks were burning in hot flames. If it weren't for the fires, the entire place would be filled with pitch-black darkness.

As soon as we had loaded into the Humvees, Barnes pulled out the detonator again. He braced himself, and then his thumb hit the trigger. The whole place went up, and a cloud of flames and smoke covered the area. Parwan was no more.

Chapter 7

The Truth

Successful Mission

From inside of the Humvee, Barnes radioed Matthew to tell him the detention facility had been destroyed. That meant that Matthew could detonate the explosives that had been planted all over the hidden village of Rharib Ail's Scasura. He was glad about that. But more than anything, he was relieved that Scarlet and the others had been found and were safe.

The village was, at this point, nothing more than abandoned ghost town ready to be erased for good. The remaining Taliban squads lay cold and dead on the ground. The women and children had been safely evacuated from the premises. Matthew and his team were at a safe distance away from village.

Matthew braced himself. He pressed the trigger and watched the entire village go up in smoke. A massive dust storm gusted through the night, filling the air with dust and sand and impeding visibility.

<hr />

When the dust began to clear, dawn had risen. We all arrived back at the base. Harry was carried out of the Humvee, since he was too weak to move. Blood was once again streaming from Kirsten's stabbed out eye. The pain she was experiencing was agony. And it wasn't just her eye. Her cracked ribs from the fall had become extremely painful. As she got out of the Humvee, Matthew and Barnes grabbed her by the waist to support her until one the medics took her.

As I climbed out of the Humvee, sunlight hit my face. An ever so gentle breeze eased the intensity of the stifling air. My bruised eye made my head ache, and my eye started to water.

Matthew and I turned to each other, and we instantly moved towards each other. Embracing, we smiled and gazed into each other's eyes and then shared a gentle, passionate kiss.

Harry Punches General Howard

After a few hours in the medical ward, Kirsten and Harry were regaining their strength. Kirsten would now have to wear an eyepatch for the rest of her life. She found it quite sexy initially. But then she started to feel unsure about it—in case it might affect her chances of finding her perfect woman.

"Just be grateful you still have both of your hands," Harry sounded frustrated as he spoke, while looking at his right wrist for the first time since the medics had treated it.

Harry thought about it. He didn't know what he was going to do; he had always been right-handed.

The medic said he would be able to get a synthetic hand fitted in a few years back home. At first Harry was disappointed that the process would take so long.

Seeing his disappointment, the medic responded to his question, "Although synthetic limbs of any kind can be made, the reason it will take so long is because your right hand is your dominant hand. Synthetic limbs that are fitted to a dominant limb have resulted in malfunctioning issues in the past."

<hr>

I was visiting the medical unit when General Howard walked in unannounced. Kirsten and Matthew stared daggers at the man. He strolled on in like nothing had happened. "Glad to see you're still here, Mr Armanton," he quipped.

Harry was fuming. Without even getting out of bed, he leaned forward and punched Howard right in his face with his left fist.

Then he got up from his bed and let his anger speak for him. "General Howard, you are one traitorous, unbalanced, psychopathic asshole. You not only betrayed me. You betrayed Scar. You betrayed Kirsten. You betrayed Matt. And you also betrayed Barnes. How could you sell us to the Taliban, huh? Was it easy for you? I bet it was, given that you're all buddy, buddy with the Taliban's second in command. You make me sick, you lying sack of shit." Harry felt out of control, but it was worth it.

After he had finished, Barnes and, surprisingly, Captain Abernathy ordered two men to drag General Howard to the brig.

But that didn't stop Howard from shouting harsh words that cut me deeply. He wished that I would die and release everyone from my spell. What he said was nonsense to everyone else. But to me, General Howard knew the truth. Liam had told him about my problem. Right now, I really wished he hadn't.

Flashbacks and Blackouts

Later on, after hearing how Harry had stood up to Howard, everyone applauded him. Tonight, all would celebrate the victory. The concentration camp and the hidden village were no more.

I sneaked away to get some fresh air. The night sky was sparkling with a billion stars shining down on me. At first, I couldn't believe that I was standing here, free from the Taliban's clutches.

Staring deep into the night, I completely tuned out the partying coming from the base. The local civilian village, a couple of miles from the base, was hustling and bustling too. I could hear snippets of singing as the villagers celebrated the return of their friends and family members who had been imprisoned in the Parwan detention facility.

The night was going perfectly. I gazed above to the stars, their sparkling reflected in my eyes. The warm muggy breeze blew into my face. My hair blowing away from me felt like it was flowing in mid-air. I embraced the soothing sensation.

Suddenly, my head felt heavy and started to throb. I forcefully squeezed my eyes shut and dug my fingertips into my temples to stop the agonising pain. As I struggled to keep it together, visions of the Mistress of Darkness and her sly smile flashed through my mind. I saw Nathaniel reaching out to me, just the way I remembered seeing him after he saved me from the well—until he dropped into the darkness.

The flashes were quick. Most of these visions never made sense. I would see things like a woman who sort of looked familiar until she transformed into the Mistress of Darkness evolves. Another recurring image was a crazy-looking man who might have been a junkie or a homeless person. But to me he didn't look like a junkie. Rather, he looked like he feared for his life, as he cowered in a corner, rocking backwards and forwards.

The more I fought, the more intense the throbbing in my head became. The endless voices echoed madly in my ears. I was filled with sheer terror at the thought that the Mistress of Darkness was still a threat to me. Sure, I had been able to break myself out of her control. But she had touched me, creating a link between us. So she was always nearby.

Matthew's Denial

Sometime later, I awoke with Kirsten's voice echoing in my ears. I mumbled her name as my vision began to clear and I regained consciousness

As Kirsten looked in my eyes, she knew I'd had another blackout and told me to tell her what had happened.

She led me to the barrack porch, where she gestured for me to sit. She went inside and returned a moment later to hand me a steaming hot flask of coffee.

"Tell me what happened and what you saw," she urged.

At first Kirsten seemed supportive and comforting. Then she started advising me that I should figure out a way to eliminate the Mistress of Darkness. What Kirsten was suggesting was too big to face on my own. I was surprised Kirsten even came up with the idea. I guess that kiss she dared me to give her had made her see what I could see.

Yet I'd kissed Matthew, and he hadn't seen any of my visions or the Mistress of Darkness.

"Maybe you grew more control when you escaped this Mistress of Darkness's dark place," Kirsten exclaimed.

I wrapped my fingers around the hot flask and sighed.

We hadn't been sitting there long when Matthew joined us, approaching cautiously and catching us off guard. He'd noticed Kirsten and I weren't at the party and excused himself to look for us. When he'd left, everyone had been cheering on Barnes as he chugged down a keg full of beer.

At first, Matthew spoke casually, joking with Kirsten about Barnes gulping all that beer down.

Kirsten glanced at me. When I nodded slightly, she got up and walked back to the party, where she planned to outdrink Barnes—she had to maintain her unbeatable reputation. She'd never taken kindly to losing, ever since she was young.

Matthew sat down next to me and gently placed his arm around me. He asked me to tell him what was wrong.

The more I explained to Matthew, the more in denial he became. It was like his brain couldn't process what I was saying.

"Wait!" he protested. "Hold on. Scar, you must realise how crazy this sounds. You're thinking about taking on a dark anomaly who no one else but you can see."

I wasn't surprised that Matthew objected to my plan. I did feel a little insulted when he referred to the Mistress of Darkness as an anomaly. But it wasn't until Matthew let slip a bit of information that Liam had told him about his secret discovery of the darkness that I started to feel confused and then angry. Knowing that Liam had hidden something from me about the darkness made my heart stop. My eyes filled up with tears, and my hands and knees trembled uncontrollably. I quickly excused myself and stood to go to my quarters.

"Scar! Wait!" Matthew said, reaching out to me.

I flicked his hand away with my right arm as I blurted out, "Don't touch me!"

◆◆◆◆◆

Matthew was taken aback when Scarlet pushed him away.

After he watched her walk hurriedly towards her quarters, he banged his fist into the wall and rested his head on his hand. He felt his heart shatter a little. He was distraught, and a feeling of guilt crept up on him. "I'm such an idiot," he said quietly.

In Need of Answers

After I stormed away to my quarters, my emotions were changing furiously—from anger to betrayal to sadness to helplessness. My heart ached because of the disagreement with Matthew.

As soon as I reached my bed, my head began to feel like it was burning. It was like my brain was on fire; it throbbed. I hurled myself onto my bed, pressing my face into my pillow, shutting my eyes tightly, and digging my fingernails dug into my temples. I began to black out, and then the flash visions began to appear.

Since I had escaped the dark place, the endless nightmares and threats from the Mistress of Darkness had died down. Now, the endless images were back with a vengeance, along with the throbbing, burning headache.

The images flashed through my mind—the same ones as always. Nathaniel's death and his voice echoing in my ears brought an endless amount of tears to my eyes.

Then the Mistress of Darkness's voice interfered; she threatened that she'd get her hands on everyone I had ever loved. I became extremely angry.

During my blackout, I appeared in a dreamlike state of paralysis in the mistress's dark place. Even though it wasn't real, I could still feel the hostility in the air.

The strangest thing was the flashlight with the encrypted messaging had been placed in my trouser pocket.

A part of me knew it wasn't the real one. The real flashlight was in my apartment back home at the base. Still, I breathed a sigh of relief, knowing I was armed against the darkness. Real or fake, light still antagonised darkness.

I knew I had to find out the truth. I had to finally try and put an end to all this.

Awakened

Inside the dreamlike dark place, I felt like I had entered one nightmare and then stepped into another, where I faced instant hostility.

I was taking on endless threats from the Mistress of Darkness, and not just verbally. She was hurling dark fiery spheres at me as well. Luckily, even with the flashlight as my only defence, I had the advantage. I was able to burn the spheres of darkness away.

With this being a dream sequence, I noticed the flashlight was equipped with a rechargeable battery and that a switch turned it to full beam, like the headlights on a car. That mode burned the darkness a lot more quickly, and the light beamed brightly.

I wasn't sure how long I had been trying to survive this nightmare I was in, but it was taking its toll on me in the real world. My body was covered in scrapes and bruises. And a head-on collision between my flashlight and her darkness had resulted in sparks that had left a pencil mark burn above my eyebrow.

Even though it was a dream, the injuries hurt like a bitch. While I slept in the real world, my hands clenched the quilt so tightly that you could see my veins and bones sticking out from underneath my skin.

The next morning, Kirsten woke up with a banging hangover headache from outdrinking Barnes. As she always said, a good hangover meant a good night.

She came to tell me about it around 10.15 in the morning. When she stepped into my quarters, to her surprise, I was still fidgeting. Ice-cold sweat dripped from my forehead, and my breathing was as rapid as it would be if I was running a marathon and struggling to breath in the process.

Kirsten rushed to my bedside and repeatedly called my name, gently shaking my shoulders.

I don't know how long Kirsten has been calling when my dream sequence self heard her voice echoing through the dark place and sensed a light shining behind me. I took one more glimpse at the Mistress of Darkness. "I'll stop you and your nightmares," I said before turning and bolting towards the light.

But the Mistress of Darkness wasn't gonna let me leave. From her hands, she summoned a clouded typhoon to drag me back to her. If it hadn't been for the flashlight, the strength of the dark typhoon would have swallowed me whole. I held it out like a beaming magic wand until I leapt into the light.

I awoke and shot up from my bed, still breathing rapidly. Ice-cold sweat was still dripping down my face.

Kirsten held me tightly, trying to comfort me.

But my mind never switched fully back from the darkness's presence. It was there, haunting me again, just like it had when I first started my journey with the military.

Kirsten insisted I go to the medic. But I couldn't. The only medic I had ever trusted was Liam. Anyone else would think I was going insane. They'd probably have me locked up or worse.

At first, Kirsten didn't seem to quite understand. She thought I was exaggerating. But as much as I knew she was trying to help, I still declined. I could never ever take that risk.

Before I could excuse myself to go to the bathroom, Kirsten asked what Matthew had wanted last night. I refused to speak about Matthew after our little disagreement. I couldn't bring myself to talk about what we had talked about last night.

<hr />

After I'd cleaned myself up and gotten dressed in some clean clothing—camouflage pants and a T-short bearing a military logo, I went to the canteen for some breakfast. Only a certain amount of food was left until the next supply run came in, which meant I had strawberry rice pudding for my breakfast. This was a breakfast I wasn't particularly fond of. Strawberries always seemed to make me gag. Even the smell of the strawberries made me want to gag. I moved the strawberries aside with my spoon.

When I'd nearly finished my rice pudding, Matthew came over. I wasn't in the mood to talk, so I asked him what he wanted quite sternly. Matthew let out a deep sigh and told me the plane that would take us home would be here in the next two hours.

I nodded, never making eye contact and kept my arms folded across my chest. Matthew wasn't stupid. He knew he had been out of line when he'd said what he said last night, especially since all he'd wanted to do was tell me how dangerous the whole idea was and that I would be taking on a big risk.

Even though Matthew said he was sorry for what he'd said, a part of me didn't want to accept that right away. At any rate, we'd stay friends and nothing more. I would never let my heart rule my head.

Flight Home

Two hours later, a specialist marine aircraft had arrived to take us back to the States—all except Barnes, Captain Abernathy, Corporal Meadows, and General Howard. The latter would remain in the brig until one of the Chinooks arrived to take him back to the States, where he'd be punished for treason.

After we loaded our stuff into the aircraft, we took a moment to say our goodbyes. Both Captain Abernathy and Corporal Meadows received handshakes, given they weren't the hugging type. Barnes, on the other hand received a bro hug from Matthew and a pat on the back from Harry, who couldn't hug properly since he was still in pain.

Kirsten and Barnes reminisced about the last time Kirsten had to leave and Barnes stayed behind. They joked and hugged each other like brother and sister.

As for me, Captain Abernathy shook my hand and then saluted for good luck. Meadows did the exact same, adding a pat on my shoulder. I walked towards Barnes. After we hugged, Barnes said gently, "Take care, Scarlet."

I nodded and gave him a slight smile before I made my way to the plane to join the others. We all turned to look behind us and saw the three men salute. We returned the salutes and then boarded the plane, watching Afghanistan outside our windows and wondering what would become of the dry desert country.

Closed Investigation

In Seattle at the police headquarters, all was quiet around the mysterious murder cases. Weeks of searching and gathering what little evidence could be found had netted nothing more but numerous conspiracy theories. The chief of police decided to close the case, due to too errors and the shortage of witnesses.

But there was one officer who wasn't the giving up type. Officer Layton dedicated most of her time to finding out who had murdered those people and to locating the mysterious woman she'd fought a few months ago.

"Listen here, Layton. The case is dead weight—no leads, no evidence, no witnesses. The case is closed," said the chief in his grizzled Southern accent.

"But, sir, the moment we turn our backs, the killer may strike again. Let's not forget, I have fought the woman who might be the killer," Layton said, her tone demanding, as she placed her fists on the chief's desk.

"A woman who is unidentifiable, just like the fingerprints on your baton," the chief retorted. Then he sternly ordered Officer Layton to leave his office.

She stormed out of the chief's office, rather annoyed and disappointed and made her way to her vehicle, where Jesse was hanging out.

To let off some steam, she decided to take Jesse to the field next to the police station and let her four-legged companion play with her tennis ball.

As the duo walked onto the field, Officer Layton let the young spaniel off her leash. The dog eyes was mesmerised by the tennis ball in her human partner's hand. Layton threw it up in the air. Then catching it again, she hurled it across the field, with the little spaniel sprinting right behind it.

A cycle of throwing and retrieving had begun. Officer Layton walked on as the dog brought back the ball, only to chase after it again and again.

Then Officer Layton stopped at a small brick wall—and gently slumped backwards, sliding to the ground and looking down at the ground with her hands on her head. She was utterly disappointed.

When Jesse returned with her ball, she dropped the ball on the ground and pushed it towards Officer Layton with her nose. But when the young dog sensed her human partner's state, she lay down next her, looking up with those big brown eyes of hers. Officer Layton gently stroked the canine's head.

Wolflike Creatures of Darkness

After the thirteen-hour flight from Afghanistan, jet lag took its toll on us. As we walked out of the plane, the sun was low in the sky, making way for nightfall.

We gathered our belongings and headed for our apartments. With a large heavy rucksack on my back, climbing the stairs was agony on my feet.

Finally, I reached my floor and walked down the long corridor to my door. I reached into my pocket for my key and opened the door. Right away, I dropped my rucksack by the kitchen and went to the bathroom to splash some water on my face to, hopefully, wake me up a little. I gathered the cold refreshing liquid in my hands and rubbed it into my face. It was quite refreshing, and I began to feel more awake. I stared deeply at my reflection. I was surprised at how more mature I looked, especially for a twenty-one-year-old. It was quite staggering.

Even after everything I'd been through and was still going through, I still saw myself as that young girl who never spoke much during elementary school. I was still that little girl who always relied on her brother, not only for protection from all the bullies, but also from someone else. I couldn't remember the details, but I knew there was someone who Nathaniel always protected me from.

It wasn't long until I made my way to my bed and fell backwards onto it. Hopefully, I could get some rest.

But the peace didn't last for long, as the echoes of voices started sounding in my ears and visions flashed through my mind. Before I knew it, I was back in the dreamlike dark place again. I was still clenching the flashlight tightly in my hand.

I gazed down at the flashlight and held it in both of my hands so that I could see the handle with the strange message on it. Some of the letters became visible—B, S, T, R, O, G, L, T, S, S. I still couldn't make out some of the letters.

My attention was suddenly interrupted when the Mistress of Darkness crept up behind me and extended her arms. A gush of darkness blasted me forward to the ground.

I quickly opened my eyes and immediately switched on the flashlight, anxiously aiming it aimlessly around me, trying to find her. But she never truly revealed herself. She remained hidden, threatening me from the shadows, though I attempted to goad her into showing herself.

The Mistress of Darkness declined and summoned four wolflike creatures made from pure clouds of darkness. The creatures charged at me. I quickly aimed the flashlight towards them, but they were fast. They knew how to dodge my attacks and surprise me with their counter-attacks.

They jumped through me like I was a ghost, making my body burn and my joints ache. The sensation knocked me to the floor. Their constant snarls and snaps echoed in my brain as they circled around me.

Before I got up, I stared into the creatures' eyes. Then I surveyed the space from corner to corner until I came up with an idea. Given that this place was a dream sequence, I could probably imagine something to help me. I knew about lucid dreaming, the most complex and unexplained part of dreaming. It was hard to explain, but focusing on what I wanted and what I needed was tricky—especially in the Mistress of Darkness's dark place.

Anything brought here would get devoured by the dark forces of this place—anything except light, which burned the darkness away. Light was the one thing darkness feared, the only source of power that weakened and could destroy it.

So I imagined something filled with light sources coming to my aid. I'm not gonna lie; trying to focus was difficult. The darkness wasn't stupid. It wasn't like this kind of thing hadn't happened before. So to distract me, the creatures started to get vicious in their attacks. But with the flashlight in my hands, I beamed the light right at them, which kept them at bay.

And then all of a sudden, right behind me, formed by sparks of light, a chest appeared. My eyes opened wide. I was desperate to get to it.

When I focused the light on one of the creatures, the light got brighter and burned it away, leaving only three of them. This angered the Mistress of Darkness. She ordered the remaining creatures to retreat. Then she appeared in front of me. And before I could see what was in the chest she pulled me towards her using her clouds of darkness—until we were directly face to face with each other.

"You're beginning to be quite the nuisance—more nuisance than advantage, in fact, young lady." I could hear the frustration in her voice, but her threats didn't scare me as much anymore.

I tried to resist.

It was then that she mentioned my mother. I instantly thought of Nicole, since she was the only proper mother figure I'd ever had. I became angry. Forcing myself out of her grip, I fell onto my back. That's what I noticed the flashlight was next to the chest. I dove for the chest.

I grabbed the flashlight, switched it back on, and aimed it at the Mistress of Darkness. She transformed into a cloud of darkness to get away from the light.

I turned my attention to the chest. What I saw stunned me to no end.

Inside the chest lay everything that could harm the darkness—road flares, flashlights, flash bangs, and even custom-made light bombs, which instantly gave me an idea. I gathered the flash bangs, flares, and a few light bombs and spread the bombs in front of me. Then I waited until the Mistress of Darkness had summoned her dark creatures again.

I could hear the snarls in the distance growing closer. I waited in the darkness until the creatures have almost reached the light bombs. Then I backed away and threw a flash bang towards them. The amount of light that illuminated the place was overwhelming. The creatures moaned like dogs in agonising pain as the light tore through them like fire to paper.

The bright light from the flash took over my vision.

I awoke from my nightmarish slumber gasping for breath. Cold sweat dripped down my forehead. I was in sheer, overwhelming shock.

A Surprise Call

The next morning, the sun was shining brightly through my window. I squinted, trying to keep my eyes open. Even without the glare, the constant struggle of being awake felt unbearable. But I forced myself to stay awake. My body felt like it had been torn apart. I constantly ached, which made me feel weak. I collapsed onto my bed.

I gradually made myself get up. I walked to the bathroom. Just like always, I had fallen asleep in my clothes. This never seemed to get to me, seeing how it kept happening.

While in the bathroom, I decided to take a nice hot shower to help wake me up. The feeling of the warm water hitting my body was so soothing. I breathed a sigh of relief. All of a sudden, being awake began to feel bearable again.

After my shower, I got dressed in my light blue designer skinny jeans and the light pink Kawasaki tank top Kirsten had given me for my birthday. I threw my light grey cardigan over the top of the shirt.

I then made my way downstairs to the cafeteria to grab myself a coffee. On my way there, I noticed Harry at the phone booth. He slammed the phone back into its cradle and, looking disappointed, buried his face into his one hand.

After a moment, I walked up to him, moving slowly. At first, Harry didn't pay attention to his surroundings; he seemed deep in his own thoughts. I gently knocked on the glass, which startled him slightly.

He laid his gaze on me and then, after a moment, walked out of the booth. He handed me a piece of paper with a phone number on it. I was confused.

When I started to ask why he had given it to me, all he replied was, "Don't worry. It's someone you know." His tone was reassuring, and he rested his hand on my shoulder.

A few moments later, I carried on to the cafeteria, and Harry went back into the phone booth. I turned and saw that he was clenching the phone tightly in his hand as he held it up to his ear.

A part of me wanted to ask him what was wrong, but I couldn't bring myself to be that nosy—even though I did have good intentions. Harry was always the type of person who kept his affairs to himself, not that anybody blamed him for being distant.

At the cafeteria, I headed straight for the coffee machine at the far end of the room. I grabbed a cup and placed it on the machine, watching as the coffee poured into the cup. When it had finished, I walked to one of the tables outside.

I sat down and put my coffee on the table. Pulling out my phone, I skimmed through my contacts, looking for a number that matched the one on the piece of paper.

Sadly, the number remained unknown. I stared back and forth between the number on the paper and my phone, wondering who would be calling me. I didn't know that many people.

As soon as the clock struck noon, my phone started to vibrate, along with emitting a poppy melodic ringtone.

I glanced for a few seconds at the number on my phone. Taking a deep breath, I answered. I couldn't have been more surprised. I wasn't expecting the voice that replied.

Hearing Nicole's voice again not only made me feel nostalgic; it also gave me a warming sensation. Even though she wasn't my real mother, she still loved me like a daughter. I still wondered from time to time, if Nathaniel were still alive, would the Fendersons love him as much as they loved me?

Nicole invited me over tomorrow to their new house in Baltimore. She and George had done some searching around about my background and about my real parents. I was intrigued. Maybe this would lead to me finding a way to finally end this endless nightmare.

I was curious why the family had moved from Washington. As I remembered it, they had been more than comfortable living in their five-bedroom terrace house.

After I said goodbye, I felt happy. I was going to see the Fendersons again. But there was one thing that worried me. And that was the possibility that the Mistress of Darkness might show up. I knew that would put them at risk. This never stopped. If the Mistress of Darkness did show up, she'd have to go through me. I would never let anyone hurt the Fendersons.

Hidden Discoveries Revealed

I was still at the table drinking my coffee when I saw Matthew gesturing for me to come over to him. I gave him an uncertain look as I walked over.

I still wasn't 100 per cent with Matthew, since he had so adamantly opposed my plan to find out more about and maybe figure out how to stop the Mistress of Darkness.

As soon as I reached him, he started to apologise for his behaviour that night in Afghanistan.

I told him accepted his apology, but I couldn't accept him anymore. Matthew accepted my answer, but inside his feelings were torn.

Right away, Matthew said he had something to show me. He said it was something that Liam had given to him, something he had discovered, which he was to give to me eventually. We walked down the corridor with no one but the cleaning staff saluting us as we walked past—all the way to Matthew's personal locker.

While Matthew retrieved this thing from his locker, I waited outside the locker room. As I leaned against the wall, I pulled my phone out of my pocket to check the time—12.31 p.m.

It wasn't long until Matthew returned with a small strongbox in his hands. We found a quiet secluded sitting area, where he handed the strongbox over to me.

I placed the strongbox on the table in front me. Then slowly I began to open it. Matthew sat directly opposite me, looking between me and the strongbox.

What I found inside the box made my interest grow. There were some notes and historical documents. But most importantly, there was my journal—the one that George and Nicole had given me on my twelfth birthday. The journal itself didn't surprise me. After all, Liam had requested that I give it to him so he could scan through it for any clues. What did catch my full attention was the fact that he had attached little sticky notes to each of the pages. This was what he had found out. The notes linked my descriptions of the darkness, the mistress, and my visions to a number of sources.

"Paranormal entity?!" I exclaimed, skimming through the notes. "Old myths, old religious legends, subconscious attacks?!" I took in a deep breath. "Liam really tried to learn about this darkness."

I sighed. "Paranormal entity," I said again, concerned. It seemed to make sense though.

Matthew remembered hearing an old Christian tale. He recalled the religious quote he had heard in Sunday school: "The light is among you for a little while longer. Walk while you have the light, lest darkness overtake you. The one who walks in the darkness does not know where he is going."

Discussing all these theories with Matthew felt warming; it helped me know that I wasn't truly alone in this situation. Even though Matthew and I would remain just friends, it was nice to have someone there. I couldn't fully rely on or trust him, even though he'd said he was wrong to have doubted me that night. While I couldn't bring myself to move our relationship forward, I wasn't blind to the fact that Matthew and I did like each other. But until the Mistress of Darkness was well and truly dealt with, I couldn't think about that. I couldn't let my emotions be a pressure point for her to use against me.

Matthew understood, but he never stopped being there for me. This made it hard for us to ignore our feelings.

I was flattered when he asked me to accompany him to the welcome home ball tonight—as friends—once I'd found out what the celebration was all about. Apparently the military threw a celebration every year when soldiers came back from wars.

I said yes, and we shared casual smiles. Matthew said he'd meet me in the parking lot outside the apartments.

Kirsten's Secret

I was heading back to my apartment with the strongbox in my hand when I bumped into Kirsten. She was getting used to some aspects of her one-eyed view, but she found it hard to concentration with just one eye.

Along with her complaints about her concentration, I noticed something else about her—something that stood out like a sore thumb. That was her beaming smile.

This piqued my curiosity quite a bit. The only time Kirsten smiled like that was when she had done something exciting. Either that or she had finally met a woman she would consider dating.

"Scar," she said, her tone serious, "might I tell you a secret?"

I was intrigued about what she had to say. "Sure, Kirsten," I said. "What's up?"

First letting out a deep sigh, she explained that she might have finally found someone. I couldn't be happier for her—especially as she had been so worried since she'd started wearing an eyepatch that it would ruin her chances to find her perfect woman.

"I'm gonna guess it's some woman who finds eyepatches sexy too," I joked.

Kirsten let out a slight laugh and then said that her new woman friend would be at the welcome home ball as her date.

A few minutes later, Kirsten and I walked to our apartments so we could get ready for tonight. I was happy for Kirsten. I knew that she would one day find the woman of her dreams.

I couldn't help but wonder if mine and Matthew's relationship would ever blossom again.

Resist

When I got back to my apartment, I closed my door and walked to the kitchen to place my key on the rack. To my great shock, Nathaniel appeared in the kitchen.

It was difficult trying not to fall for her foul trickery again. I fell onto my knees, gripping my head and digging my fingers into it. I was trying to control myself; I didn't want this to be like the last time.

This time, the mistress became more aggressive as she grew more frustrated. She was trying to break me like never before. She spat out vile and cold words, promising to harm everyone I loved if I didn't give in.

It didn't help when Nathaniel's dark form came towards me and knelt down. When he placed his hand on my cheek, I quickly moved my head away so my eyes weren't directly on him.

"No!" I cried, clenching my eyes shut. "Go away! You're not … your not …"

"You know you can't resist the possibility. Imagine you can save your brother and live your life how it should be." The mistress grabbed me by my ponytail and whispered into my ear, "Don't you want to live that life?"

"Eat shit and die, you witch," I cried.

She yanked my ponytail and scowled. Then she threw me, snickering when my face hit the floor.

I turned my head to look up at the mistress, but she had vanished into darkness. I breathed a sigh of relief.

The Welcome Home Ball

After taking a few minutes to compose myself and clear the blood from my nose, I began to get ready for the welcome home ball. Matthew, Kirsten, Harry, and I were gonna attend in honour of our return from Afghanistan.

First I cleansed myself in the bathroom. A warm steamy shower made me feel refreshed and relaxed. After getting out of the shower, I wrapped a towel around my torso and headed for my bedroom wardrobe.

Going through the formal section of my wardrobe, I felt indecisive. Then I caught a glimpse of a dress that was hidden from all my other dresses. It was a long light cream dress with sequins on the torso and a large sequin rose in the middle. I briefly remembered that Liam had gotten me this dress for my eighteenth birthday. Just thinking of that day brought a tear to my eye.

After I had done my hair in a French plait in the middle with the rest of my hair down, I got dressed. When the dress was on, I glanced at myself in the mirror. Once again, I reflected on how unbelievably old I looked for my age.

Glancing out my window, I saw Matthew leaning on the bonnet of his silver Toyota Corolla. He looked rather dapper in his black suit with his light cream waist jacket. He pulled his phone from his pocket and tapped the screen.

Seconds later, I heard the little ding of a bell alerting me to a message, and my phone lit up and vibrated. I picked it up and saw the text message from Matthew: "Are you ready, Scar?"

"Be down in a minute," I replied.

Placing my phone in my little bag and hurling it over my shoulder, I stepped into my heels and walked out my apartment.

There was a slight chill in the air, as the sun was beginning to set early, especially for mid-September.

When I made it to the car park, Matthew looked mesmerised as he watched me walk towards him.

"You look absolutely beautiful," he said, scratching the back of his head as he smiled.

"Well you look pretty handsome in that suit."

Matthew chuckled. He said no one had ever called him handsome, not even his own mother, who never gave him much support during his childhood and teen years.

On the way to the local country club where the ball was being held, Matthew felt the urge to tell me something. "I understand you must hate me after what I said, but—"

I interrupted him before he could go any further. "Matt, you clearly seemed convinced in your argument. Can we just forget about it please?" I buried my face in my hands.

<hr />

Matthew looked over at Scarlet. He felt massively guilty. He had never meant what he'd said. Ever since Liam had explained what Scarlet was going through, he could only feel sorrow for her. Even though he knew he could never fully understand everything, the most important thing was that he could be a good friend—that he could be there and support her as she faced her troubles.

With his left hand on the steering wheel, he patted her back with his right hand, hoping the touch would comfort her. "After everything you've suffered through … You've pulled through not just because of mine or Kirsten's or even Harry's support. It's because you're stronger than you look. You're basically a one-girl army. And that brother of yours, he'd be proud of you." Matthew spoke passionately. He meant what he's said.

He was happy when Scarlet slowly moved her hands from her face and looked him in the eye. He smiled gently and turned back to watch the road.

"Thank you, Matt," she said. "That really means a lot to me." He noticed that she sat up a little straighter.

<hr/>

We arrived at the country club. I held Matthew's arm as we walked towards the entrance.

We were there just in time to see Kirsten show up in her dark red SUV with her date. Kirsten wore a dark red gown along with dark red heels, and her short curly hair was brushed to one side and held in place by a red rose hair clip.

Matthew and I were very surprised at how feminine Kirsten was dressed. She was usually ruled by her tomboyish nature.

"Since when are you girl?" Matthew joked.

This earned him a disapproving look from Kirsten as she opened the passenger door for her date. She stepped out wearing a short light purple lace dress. Her long light ginger hair was laced with light pink ombré highlights.

"Scarlet, Matt, this is my lady friend, Tanya D'Reily," Kirsten said with a proud smile on her face.

Matthew and I each shook Tanya's hand as we greeted her.

Then the four of us walked into the building. We entered a large dance hall with a stage and a DJ playing all kinds of music, from pop rock to top 40 songs. There was a dance floor and several guest tables. And at one end of the hall was a long table lined with our name tags.

Harry was already here. He was standing at the bar next to the stage, drinking a large glass of scotch and gin and looking severely depressed.

We all walked towards the bar, startling Harry out of his deep depressed thoughts. He immediately snapped out of it.

Harry wore a black suit with a dark grey shirt and tie. His beard was tightly cropped, unlike his normal thick beard.

After Kirsten introduced Tanya to Harry, she decided to buy the first round of drinks.

By this time, most of the guests had arrived. Matthew was especially surprised to see his younger brother Christopher. The two of them had been very close during their childhood back in Phoenix, Arizona.

Later on, Commander Maxson Rogers and the man who was filling in for General Howard, a senior sergeant by the name of Paul Fugeley, gave welcome speeches. During this formal part of the evening, Commander Rogers and Sergeant Fugeley congratulated me, Matthew, Kirsten, and Harry for our honorary return from our heroic mission in Afghanistan.

Harry's Surprise

It was 2100. Some people were leaving, while others decided to stay a little while longer and drink, dance, and talk to us about our experiences in Afghanistan.

Kirsten spent most of the night getting to know Tanya some more. They danced together on the dance floor and even shared little kisses on the cheek.

Matthew and I shared a dance. When we finished, his brother took me aside. He told me that Matthew was a good man, which I already knew. I explained to Chris that I wasn't ready for mine and Matthew's relationship to move forward.

A woman walked in wearing a long elegant sleeveless red dress. She looked to be about thirty, and her dark brown hair fell to her shoulders.

When Harry turned to face her, his eyes widened. "Jennifer?!" He said her name gently.

***

Harry set his glass down on the bar and walked over to his fiancée, who he had been forbidden to see while he was going through his traumatic experience.

"Hello, Harry," she said softly as she looked into the eyes of her soon-to-be husband.

Harry couldn't believe it. He touched Jennifer's cheek tenderly, and she raised her hand towards his hand. They continued to look into each other's eyes.

Harry and Jennifer embraced, enjoying each other's presence and holding each other lovingly.

Harry spent most of the remainder of the night talking to Jennifer. They spoke about how he'd lost his hand. He asked if Jennifer's family still disliked him, which they had since his breakdown.

Jennifer hadn't told her family she was coming to this celebration, as they would be incredibly disappointed. They wanted her to stay far away from Harry. But seeing him now, she saw how much he'd changed. She thought back to the first time she'd seen him years ago. The man she had met during her brother's naval graduation was the man she intended to marry.

Harry simply set aside his old self. He promised Jennifer he'd make the effort to be the man she had fallen for. He couldn't imagine losing her again. He sealed that promise with a gentle, passionate, and loving kiss.

Chapter 8

The Flashlight

Faded Answers

By 2330 everyone had left, including us. Tanya and Kirsten had gone to Kirsten's for the night. Jennifer had gone home. She couldn't let her family find out she was with Harry. They would file a restraining order against him, which would destroy him.

At my apartment door, I gave Matthew a friendly hug, which he gratefully returned.

"Thank you," I said.

Matthew looked at me curiously. "For what?" he replied.

Before I entered the apartment, I turned to him and smiled. "For being so understanding," I said. Then I turned and went into my apartment.

———◆◆◆———

Matthew's heart wouldn't stop beating rapidly as he watched Scarlet disappear into her apartment. "Always, Scarlet, always," he said quietly.

Then he made his way to his apartment, the gentle smile never leaving his face.

———◆◆◆———

Inside my apartment, I changed into something more comfortable for bed. Even now, the mistress's presence was filling my surroundings. Even with the lights on, she was still around.

Suddenly, she pinned me to my bed with her clouds of darkness. While I struggled to get loose, she leaned in closer and looked me in the eye, smiling her sly smile. "Sweet dreams, precious," she whispered in my ear.

She disappeared, but the air still felt cold. Even though she was out of sight, her presence never left.

When I fell asleep, the flashes of my past appeared in front of me. The one image that stuck out to me was the same one that always did. It was the day Nathaniel died. He said something that came out muffled. I tried to make out what he was saying, but he descended into the darkness below.

Friendly Favour

The next morning, I woke up at eight in the morning, later than I usually woke up. I lay down for a few minutes, sighing with relief to be done with my usual restless night.

I got washed and dressed in a new pair of jeans and a pink Adidas hoody. Before I left my apartment, I grabbed the flashlight. Today I would visit George and Nicole. If any nasty surprises followed me, I'd be ready.

As I walked out of the apartment block, I saw Kirsten getting out of her car. When she caught sight of me, she called out, "Scar!" and walked over to me.

"Kirsten! How was your night with Tanya?" I said while we walked to the canteen.

Kirsten had one massive smile on her face. She draped her arm around me happily. Just looking at Kirsten's smile was enough to tell me that she'd had a great night. The sheer excitement in her voice and the widening of her hazel eyes told me everything.

In the canteen, Kirsten ordered two plates of apple pancakes, and I got two plastic cups of orange juice.

When Kirsten came over with the pancakes, I could smell the succulent scent of apples. It reminded of when I was ten years old. Every Saturday morning, Nicole would make apple pancakes.

I had just finished when Matthew came into the canteen to make himself a cup of mushroom coffee.

I took my plate to the cleaning conveyor belt and put my plastic cup in the bin. I called his name, drawing his attention from his coffee being made.

He turned towards me. "Hey, Scar. Did you have a good night's sleep?" he said cheerfully.

I responded with a disappointed look, and he immediately knew the answer to his question.

"Anyway, Matt, if you're not doing anything today, would you mind giving me a lift to Baltimore? I promised my foster parents, the Fenderson, I'd visit them today," I exclaimed.

Matthew agreed. He grabbed his coffee and sat with Kirsten and me. The three of us talked about last night. I realised that Harry wasn't around. He usually hung about smoking his cigarette about this time.

"Where's Harry this morning?" I asked, curious.

Kirsten also became curious when she realised Harry wasn't there for the usual routine.

"I know last night was quite a shock to him," Matthew said, wrapping his hands around his coffee mug. "He hadn't seen his fiancée for years."

After we'd been talking for a while, Kirsten had to go. She had to take a sniper exam that would allow her to remain a fully qualified marine sniper. Before she left, she turned to me. "Text me if you need anything," she said while we embraced in a friendly hug.

"I will. Thank you, Kirsten," I replied.

She walked off, raised her arms in the air, and held up her index and middle fingers. "See ya," she shouted. "Peace!"

This got a laugh out of me and Matt.

Preparations

Matthew asked when I wanted to leave. Then he caught sight of the flashlight holstered on my belt. Instantly curious, he asked me why I needed a flashlight in broad daylight.

"I'm not talking about ordinary darkness, Matt! Surely you must realise," I exclaimed.

Matthew believed me, but he never fully understood, which was why it took him so long to process.

"You're right, Scar. I realise, even though I might not understand. What I do know is that you're not the lying type. So I believe you."

There it was again—that sensation as we both looked into each other's eyes. But I instantly broke away as I felt my heart begin to shatter.

"I'm ready when you are," I said.

Matthew finished off his coffee. He got up from the chair and placed his cup on the cleaning tray on the conveyor belt.

While I waited for Matt to grab his jacket and keys from his locker, I focused all my attention on the flashlight in my hands, trying to make out the hidden letters.

It wasn't long until the flashes appeared—Nathaniel, the Mistress, and even that frightened ragged man—not to mention the constant whispering echoes.

But there was one whispering echo that stood out over all the others. They were Nathaniel's last muffled words, and they kept repeating in my head.

I didn't realise Matthew was back until he called out my name, snapping me out of my daze. I felt dizzy and nearly fell to the floor. Matthew caught me.

"Whoa, easy, Scar," he said as he wrapped his arms around me. When he looked me in the eye, he instantly knew what had happened.

"I'm okay … I'm okay, Matt," I assured him.

"Are you sure? Maybe you should rest for a bit." Matthew sounded worried.

But I wasn't gonna let this stop me. I needed more information about my past—information that George and Nicole had found and that I hoped would help me fight against the darkness.

Matt wasn't too surprised. He knew I was a fighter and that I never gave up.

I never would have thought that about myself a few years ago—when the darkness was manipulating me the first time. Back then, all I had really wanted was to end it all. I hadn't realised at first that the only reason I'd continued on was the people who cared about me and had faith in me that someday I would be strong enough to overcome my fears.

When I got back to my feet, I assured Matt that I appreciated his advice, but I had to see George and Nicole no matter what.

Matthew unlocked his car. As we climbed in, all I could think about was what George and Nichole had found out.

Watched by the Darkness

Harry sat in silence on his bed. He couldn't stop thinking about the promise he'd made to Jennifer. He had told her that he would be the same man she had fallen for, rather than the monster he had to become after he'd returned from his mission in the navy. Losing his best friend in a traumatic way had affected Harry deeply. His sergeant back then had ordered him to end his best friend's life.

Even now, Harry could still hear his sergeant's order echoing in his head. There too were the insane ramblings from his best friend as he cried out. That memory bought tears to Harry's eyes. He tried to blank it out.

Then there was the time Scarlet had fallen unconscious right in front of him. Her episode had brought the earlier traumatic experience to his mind, making it as clear as a painted picture.

———◆◆▶◀◆◆———

As Harry sat, feeling conflicted about his past, another presence was in the room, watching him like a hawk.

Only a small light shone in the room. The darkness slowly fed on Harry's fear and pain—which made him perfect bait.

———◆◆▶◀◆◆———

Harry turned to the picture of Jennifer on his bedside table. Holding it in his hand, he looked into the eyes of his fiancée.

That smile, those eyes—to Harry, Jennifer meant the world. After all this time, last night was truly something extraordinary. Her being there proved to Harry that she still loved him. She even still wore the engagement ring—even though her parents had told her not to.

No matter how much his traumatic past hurt, he still had her by his side. That was all he could ever want, even if her parents forbid them to be together. Harry understood. He was willing to win back their trust, not just for Jennifer but also to prove to himself that he would never be ruled by fear.

Family Bonds and Truths

After an hour and twenty minutes, including a slight traffic jam, we finally arrived at the Fendersons new house in Baltimore.

Before I got out of the car, I stared at the house for quite awhile. I was worried, and Matthew noticed the concerned look on my face.

"You okay?" he asked gently.

"It's been four years since I've seen them. What if they're disappointed when they see me in person?" I said.

"They can't be that disappointed if they decided to call you. At least they never forgot about you." Matthew placed a reassuring hand on my shoulder.

I felt relieved. He was right. I composed myself and then got out of the car.

Before I could close the car door, Matthew asked, "Do you want me to wait here or ...?"

I agreed for Matthew to join me.

He grabbed his shoulder bag with his personal tablet—in case there were any emergencies in need of atmospheric scanning.

We walked up to the front door. I sighed, took a calming breath, and gently knocked on the door.

To my surprise, a fully grown-up Jodie opened the door.

"Jodie?!" I exclaimed, feeling a smile coming on.

"Scarlet!?" Jodie said, with a hint of shock in her voice.

We embraced each other warmly. I hadn't thought I could love Jodie as a sister. Back when I had first arrived at their house in Washington, Jodie had been quite distant towards me. I never knew for sure why; maybe she was jealous, since she was the only girl. Or maybe she was just still in her teenage years and too stubborn to even care that much. But now it was like Jodie was in a different life. This was the first time she had hugged me properly.

She called her mother over. When Nicole laid her eyes on me, tears began to flow down both our faces. She walked over to me, placed her hands on my face, and wiped the tears from my cheeks with her thumbs. "What are beautiful young woman you've become," she said barely holding back tears.

Then she wrapped her arms around me, just like she used to whenever I had restless nights.

I introduced Matthew to Nicole and Jodie. He exchanged handshakes with both and took in some slight teasing from Jodie.

We made our way into the living room. Jodie offered to make drinks, but Matthew and I declined. We waited for Nicole as she pulled a folder out one of the end table drawers.

She handed to me. I looked at her, and then my eyes were glued to the folder. I carefully opened it.

Inside the folder, I found my profile from when I was in the orphanage and a few other notes that had been added. But the most important piece of paperwork was a copy of my birth certificate.

"How did you get this?" I asked, holding up the birth certificate.

"Well it was mostly George's idea to begin with. And Conner works in the FBI these days. He saw an opportunity since—"

"Since the FBI has files on every person in every state, all stored in its central intelligence database," Matthew said, finishing her sentence.

Nicole was surprised, until he explained that he had been with the FBI for three years.

Nicole turned back to the folder, pointing out a drawing I had done when I was eleven of the Mistress of Darkness.

Then I saw the item that stunned me most of all. There was the profile picture of my real mother—who was an exact spitting image of the mistress.

"No ... No. This can't be," I stammered quietly.

Matthew leaned forward and put his hand on my shoulder, and with my eyes glued to the picture, that was when the tears came.

Nicole got up from her seat and knelt down in front of me. She reached out to my tear-drenched cheeks. "What's wrong?" she asked me.

It took me awhile to fully answer. I felt wrong but, most importantly, hurt. Knowing that my own mother's appearance was in control of my lifelong fear sickened me.

"All this time ..." At first I spoke quietly. I was still processing everything.

Everyone in the room could see I was gonna lose it, so they tread very carefully, considering what to say.

Nicole was the first to try and say something. But before she could even get a word out I had started. "Stop!" I snapped. "Just stop. Nothing you say will make me feel any better." My anger took over, and I buried my face in my hands.

Nicole sat on the arm of the sofa I was sitting on and carefully held me in her arms, gently kissing my head as she comforted me.

After I slowly got over my shock, I finally explained my reaction to them. They were just as shocked as I was. The years before I had gone to the orphanage seemed like a lifetime ago. I tried to recall moments back then. I remembered being sheltered from someone and that Nathaniel always ended up having bruises on his face.

Finally, I picked the folder back up. Another profile picture drew my attention. Here again was another familiar face. There was only one difference. The man in the picture didn't have the long mangled facial hair and the fear in his eyes.

"I remember ..." I began, faltering.

They all turned to me. I tried to explain that the man in the picture, who the profile said was my real father, had been in my visions. "Recently, I've been having these flashbacks. They're mainly the same images that I was seeing before but with a slight twist." I paused for a second and held out the flashlight.

Luckily for me, the letters were visible to everyone else.

"I acquired this flashlight in one of my dreams. I'm not sure how, but what I theorised is that it appeared in my time of need with an encrypted message on the handle."

"What type of message is it trying to give you," Jodie asked, "like your destiny?"

Destiny!? Really? Did I look like the type of person who believed in destiny? Not in the slightest. After all the shit I'd been through and everything I'd seen, I was sure none of this had anything to do with destiny.

Nicole suggested that maybe I could find my real father. He might be the only one who could give me the full answers I wanted—if he wasn't too far gone out of his own mind.

"Even if I wanted to, how could I? I don't exactly know where he is, not to mention who he is," I said, rather disappointed.

At that, Matthew got out his personal tablet. "May I?" he asked.

When I nodded, he scanned the profile picture with the tablet's camera lens. Then we waited for his tablet to load, like waiting for a buffering online video.

Then suddenly, a fully detailed profile appeared on the screen.

"Ah!" Matthew said. "Here we go. William Alexander Jayden, an American German Jew, raised in Portland, Oregon. Just turned fifty-one last month. Currently unemployed—has been for eleven years." He looked up at me and added softly, "Since your brother Nathaniel passed away. His current address is listed as a small apartment block between Washington and Baltimore. I guess he wanted to get far away from Portland and Seattle."

I couldn't believe it. The address wasn't that far away from here. I decided to meet with my real father. Maybe, just maybe, he could answer my remaining questions.

Though given the truth that my real mother was the image of the Mistress of Darkness, I could only fear the worst when it came to what may have happened to him.

Before we left, Nicole took me aside for a moment. "Scarlet, before you go, I just want you to know that, no matter what happens, we will always love you," she said as she rested her hands on my cheeks.

Tears filled in my eyes. "I might be adopted, but the Fendersons will always be my family," I said.

Nicole burst into tears. Pulling me to her, she held me in her arms.

When we finally parted, Jodie took Matthew aside. "Be good to her," she said sternly.

Matthew responded simply, "I will," and gave her a slight nod of his head.

Jodie hugged me tightly. "Love you, little sis. Stay safe," she said gently.

This made me smile, and the tears continued to flow down my face.

Finally, Matthew and I walked back to his car. He smiled at Nichole and Jodie and then turned back to me. "That's one helluva family you've got there," he said.

"I know," I replied. "And I'm truly grateful to have them in my life."

And then we were on our way to find my real father and, maybe, the last remaining answers to the questions untold. I can honestly say I felt a sense of hope within me—for the first time in years.

Oh, Father, What happened to You?

After the short drive, Matthew pulled into the apartment block car park. It looked dark and murky, even at half past three in the afternoon. And that wasn't the only suspicious thing we saw. A door to one of the apartments had been busted down. The whole area made my skin crawl, and goosebumps appeared on my arm.

"I'd keep that flashlight out at all times," Matthew said cautiously.

As we got out of the car, I quickly switched the flashlight on and walked inside the apartment block with Matthew close behind. We made our way slowly up the stairs, glancing from corner to corner. Paranoia was slowly creeping through our minds.

When we reached the fifth floor, we heard sobbing coming from the second door on the right side of the hall.

We headed towards it. Matthew decided to keep watch at the door, while I entered slowly with the flashlight in my hand. The sobbing died down and was replaced by insane, frightened rambling.

After quickly checking the front rooms, I entered the bedroom. There I saw a man cowering in the corner, clenching a photo frame in his hands.

As soon as he laid his eyes on me, he flinched, letting out a scream. "No!" he cried. "Away foul evil darkness. I see what you're trying to do." He reached for the large wax candle on the bedside table, which was lit, and charged at me.

Hearing the commotion, Matthew rushed in. When he got to the bedroom, he saw me pinned to the floor with a crazed William trying to burn me with the candle.

"Hey!" he shouted. "Get off her." He grabbed William by his tattered dark blue shirt and threw him to the floor away from me.

I sighed with relief. I had been struggling to get my real father to release his grip on me, to no avail.

After Matthew helped me up, I knelt next to William. Hoping to show him I wasn't the darkness, I raised a hand and flashed the light from my flashlight onto it. His fear slowly disappeared.

But denial crept in. "You're lying!" he cried. "The darkness wants me to reveal where my children are. *No!* I may be a broken-hearted man, but you shall never break my spirit." William spoke boldly, trying to defend the secrets he knew.

Trying to convince him was difficult. So I listened as he spoke about his beloved wife, Justine, who had fallen upon her fears and became highly overprotective when their third child was born.

I was confused. It was just me and Nathaniel. We didn't have any other siblings. Cautiously, I asked about the third child.

This didn't please him. "Don't play dumb with me, you foul woman. You know about my second child—my stillborn son," he said angrily, brandishing the candle at me.

Learning that I would have had another big brother shocked me to the core. I reflected back to my childhood, suddenly remembering that Nathaniel would always be in mourning on the thirtieth of January. He wouldn't speak. But the part of the memory that stuck out most was what happened during the night. Justine would constantly bang on his bedroom door, shouting and crying. Nathaniel would lean against the door to stop her.

I was desperate to find out more, even if he was being protective. I had to tread carefully to get the information I needed.

"Mr Jayden, you need too listen to me. I only want to help. I can stop the darkness but only if you can help me," I said softly, trying to gain his trust.

William's Thoughts

William would never forget that terrible day in the '90s. Nor would he forget the awful late afternoon a few years later when he told the social worker to remove Nathaniel and Scarlet—to take them away from his bewitched wife.

To this day, he questioned what life would be like if his stillborn son had been born alive and healthy—if he was here, rather than buried deep beneath the soil. Why? It was a question William frequently asked himself.

Why did his wife fall victim to fear from pain and loss?

Why did this fear destroy his family, curse his entire existence, and break his soul until he was nothing more than a complete wreck?

Before this nightmare, William had been a well-known Jewish photojournalist. He had befriended one of the richest families in California, who respected him and hired him for his photography skills for their personal celebrations and public outings.

His photos had helped kick-start the modelling and theatrical career of the family's oldest daughter, Justine Elisabeth Calloway. During the time when they were both working on Justine's portfolio, they had fallen deeply for one another.

William kept reminding himself of those good old days, like the day they'd announced they were together to both of their families. Then there was the surprise engagement party on the sandy beach in California. Justine had worn a gorgeous wedding dress on their wedding day. William remembers clearly how mesmerised he had been when he'd seen the woman he truly loved and how happy he was to call her his wife.

Now, William knew, all those memories in his head were just that—memories. They were memories of the days when he was happy, instead of living in constant fear like he was now. The only relief he had now was imagining what his life would be like if none of this had ever happened. Would he still be deeply in love with his beloved wife? Would he have a good relationship with his children? He especially thought of his youngest child, the daughter who he hadn't seen much of. During the time Justine was giving in to the darkness, she had forbidden William to see the children, afraid he would take them away and that she would lose them, like she'd lost their stillborn son.

As he thought of those days, William started to realise something. He looked at the young woman holding the flashlight in her hand, and then he looked into her sapphire blue eyes—the same colour as his. And then he realised who she was.

The shock was unreal. As he took this fact in, tears slowly dripped down his rugged bearded face. He reached out to her.

"Scarlet?" he said. "My Scarlet!"

The Key to the End

After William realised that I was his daughter and called my name, he stared at me, speechless. I raised my hand to touch his and smiled at him.

Only then did he wrap his arms around me. Tears rushed down his face as he savoured the feeling of comfort and love he felt embracing his now fully-grown daughter.

"Look what a beautiful young woman you've become," he said with a smile. I would learn that it was the first smile that had crossed his face in years.

William then turned his attention to the flashlight and offered to look at it. I gladly allowed him to. When his hands came into contact with the handle, a flood of memories flowed through his head. He remembered using this very same flashlight when he fought the darkness.

"This was my mine, only the encrypted message is different," he said with surprise in his voice.

"Wait," I said. "This belonged to you." I was surprised, though I supposed it made sense that it had come to me from him.

William explained that, after Nathaniel and I had been taken to the orphanage, he had gone back to the house to confront her. As soon as he'd laid his eyes on hers, he had known she was no longer the woman he'd fallen in love with.

He had slowly pointed the flashlight towards her, saying the words she had said in her wedding vows to him. "Forever I'll love you." As he spoke, he flipped the flashlight on, and the letters forming those words appeared on the flashlight's handle and lit up with sparks of light.

The light beamed towards his bewitched wife. She flashed a beam of darkness back at him. The light and dark collided. Instead of moving towards her, William made a quick escape through the window. He landed on the bottom part of the roof. And seconds before the house faded into darkness as a result of fighting the agonising pain from the light of the flashlight, which remained inside it, he leaped onto the road. From there, he watched, exhausted, as the house he and Justine had bought faded away into the darkness—as if it had never existed in the real world.

"So I have to remember what Nathaniel said before he died for the flashlight's light to penetrate her?"

William nodded. But there was a catch. There was a possibility that I wouldn't make it out alive, and even if I did, it wouldn't be easy.

It took awhile for that piece of information to sink in. I hadn't expected to go up against this fear that had taken over my real mother. And I expected that I would have to die along with it just to stop it.

William felt sorrow when he told me the news, but he understood what I had been through. He understood the horrendous nightmares and the hallucinations that led to the constant paranoia. He understood the manipulation of the darkness and the horror of doing its bidding. I felt so ashamed to bring that part up. But hearing that William had gone through the same thing and refused to continue mid-trial was comforting. At least I wasn't the only one.

"If you plan to take the darkness on, I might have a few things for your friend—if he wants to help you." William opened the damaged wardrobe and pulled out a large steamer trunk.

"Matt's not the only one helping me."

William was quite surprised but gladly accepted it. He had closed himself off from his circle of friends. He worried that his friends would be at great risk. He warned me about the danger. If any of them showed any kind of fear, the darkness would sense it and feed off it. Their fear would make them perfect bait.

When William opened the steamer trunk, I was stunned. Not only did the trunk contain flashlights and batteries, it also had flares, flash bangs, bombs, and light firearms powered by micro-fusion batteries just like the flashlights.

"When you get to Seattle on north Holgate Street, stand on the empty plot where the house used to be. Hold the flashlight to your chest. Close your eyes. Think about what you want to appear. And switch the flashlight on. As soon as you open your eyes, the house will appear. This flashlight is the only way to flash travel. So it's the key that will allow you to access the dark gloomy place where it now resides."

William finished packing all the necessary gear into a large duffel bag. He handed it to Matthew, who'd offered to carry it.

Just before we left, my phone started ringing. I looked at the screen and saw it was Kirsten, which concerned me.

When I answered, Kirsten was in a panic. She was talking about Harry attacking her like he was possessed. I worried that the darkness had gotten to him.

"Sit tight, Kirsten. We're on our way," I said reassuringly, trying not to let her pick up on my hint of worry.

"It's not like I'm going anywhere," she said. "Also, you better hurry."

Kirsten was inside a broom closet. Nearby, a darkness-enraged Harry was barging through a door and coming to find her.

The Darkness Speaks to Harry

A few hours earlier, Harry had been in a world of doubt. The troubles he'd faced in his past had crept up on him. He didn't know that it was the Mistress of Darkness manipulating his mind. Everything flooded back to him—his sergeant's orders, his best friend's insane rambling, his fellow soldiers trying to make him feel better. Influenced by the darkness that Harry was powerless to stop, their words twisted into negativity.

The more he tried to ignore it, the louder and more terrible the voices got. Soon it was the voices of Jennifer's family, threatening him and ordering him to stay away.

Though some of the voices were true—things people from his past had actually said—Harry knew the rest were fake. He tried to block it all from his mind. *Why is this happening to me?* he asked. *Why won't it stop?*

How can I make it stop? Harry thought over and over as he stumbled to the bathroom to wash his face in the sink.

After splashing his face with cold water, he looked up to the mirror and saw a friendly face behind him. Little did he know, it was something far more sinister than he could have imagined.

"Jennifer?!" he said with surprise in his voice. He quickly moved towards her.

Before he could place his hand on her hip, she placed her hands on his cheeks. She whispered sweet nothings of sugary soothing poison, convincing him it was going to be okay, if only he trusted her.

The darkness had lured Harry by using his fiancée, the one person who he loved more than anything in the world. The darkness played along and gently kissed Harry on the lips with the face of Jennifer. Harry didn't hesitate. At the moment their lips had touched, the darkness fully engulfed him and took control.

Possessed Harry Attacks

Kirsten was getting concerned. Harry was still nowhere to be found around the base. She decided to go to his apartment to see if he was all right.

When Kirsten knocked on his door, there was no answer. Not a single sound could be heard. Noticing that the door was unlocked, she opened it slightly, peaking in to see if he was in there.

Her worry grew when she saw that the whole room was in pitch-black darkness. Only slight rays of light coming from the window cut through the darkness.

Kirsten pulled out her phone and switched on the flashlight. Quietly and delicately, she entered the room. Then she called out Harry's name and frantically pointed the light from her phone into every corner of the room. Kirsten was getting rather paranoid. She felt a spine-chilling coldness in the air. Goosebumps appeared on her arms and back.

Just as Kirsten went to enter Harry's bedroom, she was ambushed. Harry rushed to her and grabbed her by the neck, pinning her against the wall.

"Where is Scarlet Jayden!" he screamed. "She needs to suffer for what she did!" Harry's voice was angry and slightly distorted.

Kirsten struggled to release herself from Harry's grip, which was nearly impossible. He didn't seem like himself. There was only one theory that came to her, and it terrified her.

Frustrated, Harry lifted her by her neck and slammed her onto the breakfast bar.

"Harry, snap out of this fucked-up creepy horseshit," Kirsten yelled. She grabbed his wrist and punched him in the face, making him lose his grip on her neck and tumble backwards.

Unfortunately for Kirsten, Harry made a quick recovery. The darkness within him made a machete-like blade appear at the end of his arm in place of his missing hand.

"Oh that's so unfucking fair," Kirsten said, dodging Harry's constant slashing, which backed her into a corner.

Before Harry could drive his machete hand into Kirsten, she grabbed his wrist to push him back. The attempt was unsuccessful, since he was stronger than her. But before he could extend the blade further Kirsten kicked him in the stomach, knocking him off his feet. Kirsten quickly picked up her phone and pointed the flashlight at him.

But it was nowhere near as effective as a normal flashlight. The light only slightly burned, and the darkness within Harry screamed a ghostly echo and then brushed aside the pain.

Kirsten wasted no time in getting out of the apartment. She slammed the door shut, hoping it would slow him down. She spotted the broom closet next to the stairs. When Harry stabbed the blade through the apartment door, Kirsten let out a muffled scream.

She ran to the broom closet. She could hear Harry calling her name as he sliced the door to his apartment, slowly and methodically shredding it to pieces.

From inside the broom closet, Kirsten rang Scarlet to tell her what was happening. As she waited for her to answer, she could only hope she would be safe until Scarlet and Matt could get here.

<hr />

After receiving the call from Kirsten, I let Matt know that we had to go—now. I said my thanks and goodbye to William, and Matthew and I rushed back to the base, praying that we weren't too late.

It took us less time to get back to Washington DC than it had taken us to get there. As soon as we arrived, I flew out of Matthew's car, grabbing an extra flashlight for Kirsten to defend herself with, and headed into the apartment block, with Matthew running behind me.

Harry had torn the door to his apartment completely down and he was searching for Kirsten. When he saw me, he came charging at me like a bull out of a gate. Before I could pull out the flashlight, Harry had hold of me by the throat. He lifted me up and slammed me to the ground.

Matthew went to knock him down, but Harry was one step ahead. He grabbed Matthew's arm and swung him, flinging him through the doorway and to the back of the room.

Matthew was down. The darkness possessed Harry, and let out a little chuckle as he raised his arm, the blade at its end pointing at me. He was about to drive it into me. "Once you're dead, everything will be back to normal," Harry said in his distorted voice. I immediately recognised the mistress's voice in the background.

While struggling to keep the blade away from me, I tried to snap Harry out of it. I knew all too well what had happened. "Harry! You have to listen to me. You have to fight it. You have to wake up," I pleaded.

But the darkness that was in his mind fought against my words, and Harry couldn't resist.

Kirsten, who had been peering at the scene from her hiding space, saw that the flashlight had dropped from my belt. She burst out of the broom closet and dove to grab it. But the darkness around Harry blasted Kirsten backwards towards Matthew.

I was able to kick Harry off of me and knock him to the ground.

When Kirsten and Matthew came round and emerged from the doorway, I gave the extra flashlight to Kirsten.

"Never thought I would fight with a damn flashlight," Kirsten said as she glanced at the flashlight.

Harry charged towards me. Just before he grabbed me again, Kirsten switched on her flashlight and aimed it at Harry. The light burned him. The darkness tried to shield him, as the pain it felt was intense.

Matthew passed extra batteries to Kirsten, but Harry moved as swiftly as a jet. Matthew and Kirsten tried to defend each other, but Harry grabbed first one and then the other by the neck, throwing them down.

He then charged at me and grabbed me by the waist. We both fell over the railing. Lucky for me, I held onto the stair railing. Adrenaline filled my veins, and sweat poured from my forehead as I tried to simultaneously pull myself up and dodge Harry's attacks from below.

Matthew was the first to come round. Seeing my flashlight next to the stair railing, he stumbled over. That's when he saw me hanging on and Harry charging back up the stairs.

"Hey, Scar, catch!" Matt shouted as he dropped the flashlight down to me.

I caught it and aimed its beam directly at Harry, causing him to stumble over the stairs.

I swung my body forward so I could jump on the stairs, where I confronted the darkness-possessed Harry.

"I don't want to fight, my friend," I cried. "You foul mistress, let him go! Harry, please, you must be strong. I know you are better than this." I had to convince him to fight against the darkness.

In the back of my mind, the words I had said—*be strong*—triggered something. I remembered the day Nathaniel died. Suddenly, what he had said became clear. "Be strong, little sis."

When I again pointed my flashlight at Harry, I spoke those words. The letters on the handle lit up, spelling out the phrase and igniting like sparks. And the light beamed brightly. The darkness within Harry began to separate painfully from his body. Both he and the darkness screamed in agony.

After the darkness separated itself from him, he fell to his knees. I knelt down next to him.

"I'm sorry, Scarlet. I'm so sorry," he said.

He hugged me tightly, and I returned his embrace and forgave him, feeling only sympathy.

But it didn't end there. All of a sudden, enraged by the massive disappointment, the Mistress of Darkness chose to end Harry's life. She stabbed her blade-like arm straight through his back.

An expression of shock filled his face, and he stuttered. He tried to grab onto me with his hand. Then he lost control of his limbs and, finally, collapsed to the ground.

I held onto his shoulders. "No, no," I cried. "Harry, stay with me. You're gonna be okay. You'll make it through. Harry, please stay with me ... Please. You can make it through." Tears slid down my face as I watched the colour drain from his face.

Kirsten and Matthew knelt down besides me as I held Harry, trying to convince him not to give up.

"It's too late, Scar, it's too late," he managed to say. "I'm sorry for being so ... distant. You're a bright, honest, kind, and caring young lady. But before I pass I have one request." He wheezed. "Tell Jennifer ..."

But the sentenced remained unfinished. He was gone.

I was completely devastated. Harry's death was terrible. And I thought, too, of how Jennifer would react when she found out.

Tonight was truly a heartbreaking night. Tears of sadness flowed down our faces, drenching our cheeks. This had to end once and for all.

Chapter 9

Decisions

William's Upcoming Demise

After Scarlet and her friend Matthew had dashed out to take care of something, the air in the room had filled with that bone-chilling coldness that was all too familiar. Then William heard the sweet poison whispers of his bewitched wife.

"I know you're here, Justine. Or should I call you Mistress of Darkness?" William spoke more confidently than he normally did.

The mistress felt insulted that William showed no fear—he hadn't made even the slightest stutter when he spoke. "Oh now, you disappointment me, my love," she said as she appeared in front of William, slowly stroking his cheek.

Her words sounded so sweet it made his skin crawl. Her voice oozed sex and cold violence. "Du machst mir keine Angst, Hexe," William said in German. He grabbed her wrist, pulling her hand from his face and stared angrily into her eyes.

The intense conversation lasted a few hours. The mistress tried to break him again. But William was already broken. His family had been torn apart, and he had lost the life he only wished he could have had.

"Fick dich." He spoke his final words confidently, a stern but serene expression on his face.

The mistress, enraged by his courage against her, formed her blade-like arm and drove it through William's chest. She watched as the colour slowly drained from his face and he slowly sunk to the floor. She knelt over him as he lay on the floor, still in shock from the fatal wound. He had already lost a severe amount of blood. The mistress sealed his death with a kiss on his lips.

"This had to be done, my love. Our daughter has corrupted you. And just like you, she will fall," said the mistress coldly before she transformed into a cloud of darkness.

The Long-Awaited Journey Home

Still traumatised from Harry's death, I felt like I was to blame for all of this. I felt nothing but endless guilt. The tears streamed from my eyes continuously.

Matthew told Kirsten to escort me back to my apartment, but I was resistant. The fire in my eyes flared. This time, the darkness had finally pushed me to the edge. All I wanted was to end this. I grabbed my flashlight and headed out of the apartment block. Kirsten and Matthew both bolted towards me, trying to stop me. But I ended up taking my anger out on them.

"Scar! Wait. You can't go after that witch of darkness like this." Kirsten grabbed my arm.

"Get off me, Kirsten. I will not endanger you more than I already have," I said as I pulled myself from Kirsten's grip.

I was so distraught I couldn't think of anything, except that I couldn't allow Kirsten and Matthew to get in my way. This was my fight, and it needed to end, sooner rather than later.

Matthew stood in front of me. He placed his hands on my arms. "You think you can take on a dark paranormal entity in this emotional state? You'll be more vulnerable than ever. I'm sorry, Scarlet," he pleaded. "You can't. I know it's a death sentence. And if it isn't, your mind will be fried."

"Does it look like I care anymore?" I snapped. "You have no idea how this feels for me. I will not put you two in harm's way for me." I looked directly into his eyes and then turned to Kirsten, doing the same. I had to convince them I was right.

First Nathaniel and then Liam and now Harry. I began to wonder if I was cursed. I might as well be. Given everything I had been through, it felt like my life was one big nightmare that was never gonna end—unless I ended it.

———•◦✕◦•———

Matthew and Kirsten were scared, but most importantly they understood that Scarlet was going to face what would amount to a death sentence.

Kirsten had never believed in anything paranormal or subscribed to superstitious nonsense—not until she'd had that kiss from Scarlet. That had made her a believer. She could never imagine going through anything like that herself. She found it heart-wrenching.

For his part, Matthew was at a crossroads. The moment Harry had died, he knew Scarlet was never gonna change her mind about confronting the darkness. And he admired her determination. But he knew that could losing the only woman he loved. His heart ached just thinking about the possibility.

———•◦✕◦•———

"Scarlet, wait!" Kirsten shouted.

I stopped in my tracks and felt a slight smirk cross my face. "No offence, Kirsten, but you're still not gonna change my mind," I said as I slowly turned around.

She and Matthew were standing next to each other.

"Yeah, we know. But were not gonna let you go alone."

Matthew's words made me hesitate. I spoke of the dangers that we might face, but they continued to stick by me.

"We're with you, Captain Jayden," Kirsten said jokingly, patting my shoulder.

I was worried but humbled at the same time. I embraced two of the closest and dearest friends I had ever had. In fact, I could hardly believe that I did have them.

Before we could leave, we still had the matter of Harry's body lying on the ground next to the stairs. Matthew said he'd stay with Harry's body while he rang the paramedics and alerted Commander Rogers and Sergeant Fugeley.

Meanwhile, Kirsten and I went to the trunk of Matthew's car to inspect the gear that would be needed. Kirsten's eyes widened with excitement as she held one of the light firearms William had given us. It looked like a light machine gun, only with slight differences—like the ammunition drum; instead of being loaded with bullets, it was powered by micro-fusion batteries.

"Oh I think I'm in love," Kirsten said, in a voice that suggested she was sexually attracted to this firearm. It reminded me of the way she'd talk about her sniper rifle, Sandy.

"Don't get too attached, gun nut," I teased as I watched Kirsten admire the fabulous firearm, inspecting its every detail.

A few hours later, the police and paramedics had arrived. After the police had investigated Harry's body, they'd placed a large blanket over the body. One of the paramedics had contacted the coroner so the body could be removed from the premises.

Watching Harry's dead corpse be zipped inside a body bag had been gut-wrenching. Guilt had crept through me again, despite how much I tried to tell myself that it wasn't my fault. It seemed the more I told myself that, the more I felt that agonising guilt that simply would not go away.

Once the police and paramedics left, along with the coroner, Sergeant Fugeley took us aside. He asked us politely to break the news to Jennifer delicately, which crushed our spirits. The news would devastate her. Learning that the man she loved more than anything in the whole wide world was gone would tear her apart. And all the promises he had made about being the man she had fallen in love would be nothing more than a heartbreaking memory that would never become true.

After Sergeant Fugeley walked away, Matthew turned to me. "Well, Captain Scarlet. Is it time to move?"

"Let's finish this nightmare together," I said.

Kirsten and Matthew nodded. We formed a circle and each extended our right hands towards the middle, one on top of the other—in memory of our fallen friends.

"For Harry," Kirsten said.

"For Liam," Matthew said. He turned and smiled at me as he laid his hand on top of Kirsten's.

I let out a deep sigh. "For Nathaniel," I finally said, laying my hand on top of Matthew's.

We nodded in unison.

Kirsten offered to drive us in her dark red SUV, seeing how it carried more fuel and was more suitable for long journeys. Also it had more room for the duffel bag with all the gear we'd need. I climbed in the front, and Matthew got in the back with the duffel bag.

A vinyl outline of two sexy beach women in silhouette faced each other from each corner of the rear window.

Neither Matthew nor I were surprised. We knew that Kirsten sure liked her women. *Typical Kirsten*, we both thought.

——◆◆◆◆◆——

Our journey to Seattle was long and, most importantly from my perspective, scary. I knew I would give my life to end it all. But though if felt dutiful, it also seemed like kind of a waste, dying at twenty-one; it wasn't exactly the best age to go out.

But I knew that I could make a difference and, perhaps, rid the world of this darkness. I envisioned burning it with the bright light of a flashlight—even to me it sounded insane and unrealistic. But if that was what it took, I would do it. I believed it even if I was really insane.

On every highway, through state after state and one rest stop after the next, I had felt myself finally breathing easier. Now the moment was getting much closer—only a few more miles left. The tension was slowly building up. My heart was pounding rapidly. My veins were visible through my skin as my blood boiled inside of me.

There were moments where she'd talk to me, trying to persuade me to give up and saying I'd accomplish nothing. She spoke coldly, her presence within me digging its fingernails into my mind.

But I had changed. I was no longer afraid. The only thing that scared me now was the realisation that, if the darkness won, she'd probably find another victim to manipulate. I couldn't let that happen. I wouldn't. I would fight until there was not a breath left in me.

——◆◆◆◆◆——

When we finally made it to Seattle, Kirsten parked in a lot next to a few closed-up convenient stores, five minutes away from North Holgate Street.

Kirsten and Matthew selected their weapons—each took light firearms, as well as a few flares, some flash bangs, and a few of the light bombs. I only took five flares; three flash bangs; and, of course, the flashlight with the message clearly visible on the handle. As I glanced at it, a few tears slid down my cheeks.

Matthew took out his personal tablet with the atmospheric scanner plugged in, and we walked down the street. As we got closer to the lot, Matthew's tablet started acting up. The air became chilly. The presence of the darkness itself got even closer when we stood directly in front of the empty lot next to two abandoned houses.

"This it. I can feel it," I said as I took out my flashlight and held it to my chest, just like William had said I should.

I then shut my eyes tightly and switched on the flashlight.

When I opened my eyes again, I saw that it hadn't worked. I was confused. How was I supposed to summon the house?

Matthew had a suggestion. "William said that, as soon as he escaped, the house faded away due to the amount of pain the darkness was experiencing from the flashlight. Maybe you need to point the beam of the flashlight in the direction where house was to summon it. Otherwise, it might flash travel you to the mistress's dark place."

What Matthew's theory entailed was quite fascinating. Maybe it had been a lot simpler when William had faced the mistress.

Kirsten, though she hadn't been with us when we met William, took in everything we were saying and came up with her own suggestion. "Let me get this straight. Instead of the darkness within the house coming to you, rather, you'll be going into the dark lair where the house lies?"

Kirsten's summary made sense. With the house having been hurled into the mistress's dark place after William bailed out, it was unable to penetrate the barrier that led into this realm, where it no longer exist.

I took a breath and pointed with the flashlight. I closed my eyes and switched on the flashlight again. In what felt like light speed in space, the light seemed to penetrate the clouds of darkness, and we reached the house.

As soon as I opened my eyes, I was struck by memories of Nathaniel and me playing together. I remembered him teaching me how to draw when I was about five. The memories were distracted by the wolves of darkness and the hostile clouds that would easily penetrate your body and cause never-ending pain.

After we took care of the dark attackers, I was faced with a dilemma—I had to decide whether to sacrifice myself or find a way to survive this last stand.

Sacrifice

(Continue to read on—Chapter 10a)

Survive

(Skip to Chapter 10b)

Chapter 10a

Sacrifice

Just before I entered the house, Kirsten and Matthew took me aside. The devastation on their faces was more than enough to tell me how they felt about this.

First Kirsten came to me and wrapped her arms around me, tears filling her eyes. "Good luck, Scar," she said. "Promise you'll try and make it out alive."

Kirsten's words hit me hard, as I couldn't make that promise. "Oh, Kirsten, you know I can't make a promise I can't keep. I'm sorry," I replied.

She buried her face into my shoulder. That started the tears flowing from my eyes. I welcomed Kirsten's embrace.

Matthew had remained silent through Kirsten's goodbye. He'd simply watched on, scratching the back of his head down to his neck, his heart aching.

Kirsten gently kissed my forehead. Just then, more of the dark attackers appeared. When Kirsten turned to engage them, Matthew stepped towards me.

"Do what you have to do," he said as he placed his hands on my arms.

I met his gaze, and we leaned into each other for one quick final kiss. The sensation felt out of place.

For Matthew, the chance to hold Scarlet was good. But it was also upsetting. He hadn't told her how he felt. If Scarlet died, he'd never get a chance to tell her he loved her.

No sooner had they stepped apart than one of the four-legged carnivores of darkness pounced on him. Pinning him to the ground, it snarled and snapped. He grabbed his flashlight from his belt and shined it on the creature of darkness. Looking up, he saw that Scarlet was using her flashlight to help burn the creature off of him.

When he got up, he turned to her with resolve. Grabbing hold of his light firearm, he cried, "Go! We've got this."

With that, he dashed to Kirsten's side to help her fight more of the dark attackers.

***

The door, it seemed, was protected by darkness. I shined my light onto it, burning it away amid screams of agony.

As I entered, I could hear endless echoes of cries for help. "Let's us go," the voices called. "Somebody help us. Let us go." I heard this words over and over again as I made my way up the stairs. I realised these voices belonged to the souls of her victims, who were being kept here by force instead of being at rest. I also realised I could hear Nathaniel's voice among them.

"I'm coming, big brother," I said quietly. "I'm here to set you free."

I searched the first few rooms for the mistress. One room in particular sparked a ton of memories. I had visions of playing together with Nathaniel and how he would never let me out of his sight. I recalled the banging on the door and the shouting that seemed endless. And I saw how he had vigilantly kept the door closed and the countless beatings he'd endured as a result.

As I exited the first bedroom, I made my way into the master bedroom across from the room I was in—the room where the mistress resided.

The moment I laid eyes on her, I thought I was in one of my dreams again. This moment felt terrifyingly surreal. When she spoke, I had to assimilate the new knowledge I had gained—this was the face of my mother, and that made me sick to my stomach.

"At last we see one another, in person," she said as she walked slowly towards me.

But before she could touch me, I pushed her back and pointed the flashlight at her. "Don't try it. You manipulated me before, but never again. You're finished," I said aggressively.

In response, she chuckled slightly, as the darkness sensed my anger.

She then blasted me to the wall, appearing in front of in an instant flash of darkness. She lifted me up by the throat. "All that fear, now replaced by anger," she said coldly. "You know this would have ended long ago if you hadn't fought against me in your trials."

I tried to resist her harsh words.

It was then that we were interrupted by the wailing echoes of her victims and the brief hovering appearance of faces—images of souls kept in the darkness.

Disturbed and horrified, I asked about the echoes.

She smiled slyly. "Most are my victims and previous faces I've worn over my years on this earth. I survive through nightmares and shadowed thoughts—like those of your poor weakling of a mother, who just wanted to never let you go after her second child died. Instead, she was branded dangerous and unstable."

"That's why Nathaniel sheltered me from her."

She slammed me against the wall, holding her face in front of mine. "That brother of yours was nothing more than an overprotective nosy little swine," she snarled.

After she said this I had lost—my cheeks burned with the rage that was flaring up inside me. "Don't you dare say anything about my brother, you monster," I screamed. I kicked her with both legs, and she flew backwards across the master bedroom. Not bothering to catch the breath her tight grip had taken from me, I grabbed a flash bang from my belt. I hurled it at her as I leapt forward to grab the flashlight.

When the flash bang exploded right in front of the mistress, the flooring throughout the house began to crack and fall apart. I leapt over to the landing next to the stairs and grabbed hold of the first bedroom's door handle. I hung on as the floor beneath me fell apart.

Once the mistress had recovered from the agonising pain of the flash bang, she transported herself with the darkness from the master bedroom to the doorway from which I hung, clinging to the door handle. She chuckled, readied her hands, and fired her darkness towards me.

I switched on my flashlight to shield myself from her darkness. The moment the light made contact with the darkness, it screeched in agony. But it toughened up and took the pain.

Then the mistress shot the door handle I was hanging onto. The blast struck my hand, and I let go, falling to the crumbling floor beneath me.

She shifted into a cloud of darkness, almost as if she had done a quantum leap. Just as I was about to get up, the Mistress appeared in front of me and slapped me across the face, knocking me back down.

"You know what. I think I've found my new face." She smirked.

Recovering from her slap, I could see the flashlight in front of me. I carefully crawled to it.

When she noticed what I was doing, she blasted me away with darkness, taunting me and gloating at my pain.

I was on my knees, and my head began to throb from the blast. But that wouldn't stop me. I jumped up and charged towards her, diving for her waist so I could knock her down.

Instead, I flew through her as if she were a ghost.

I caught sight of the flashlight on the floor next to me. I grabbed one of the flares I had on my belt. Just as I lit it, the mistress blasted me with her darkness again. I dropped the flare on the floor and burned the darkness severely as the spark from the flare burned brighter and brighter.

I quickly composed myself and scooped up the flashlight. Pointing it, I quietly spoke out Nathaniel's last words: "Be strong, little sis." The letters on the handle ignited, sparkling with light, and the light beamed brighter than the flare.

Considering how much pain she was in, I was surprised that the mistress continued to fight. She fired her darkness, and the light and darkness collided. I gradually moved towards her. When we were close enough to make direct eye contact with each other, I swapped the flashlight into my left hand and pulled my last flash bang out. Before I dropped it, I closed my eyes and spoke my final words.

"Goodbye, Matthew," I said quietly.

The flash bang dropped from my hand. I wrapped my arms around the mistress, switching the flashlight back into my right hand so I could continue to aim it at her. When the flash bang exploded, the light got brighter than ever before, and everything started to burn.

———◆◆✕◆◆———

Outside the house, Kirsten and Matthew continued to fire at the dark attackers. The pain they felt when one of the dark creatures went through them was agonising. But they continued to fight.

Suddenly, light from the house became extremely bright. The attackers began to split into pieces as the light pierced their skin as if it were paper. They screeched in sheer pain.

Matthew thought of Scarlet in there. His heart began to rule his head. He called out her name and made to run into the house. But Kirsten stopped him. She grabbed him by the shoulder and pushed him down. Together, they ducked, shielding themselves just as an earth-shattering bang slammed through the air, almost like a sonic boom. The explosion created a powerful wind current that sent them flying back across the now empty property lot. The light had burned away the darkness.

When Matthew opened his eyes, he centred his glasses on his face. "We're ... We're alive?!" he said with surprise in his voice as he stood up and looked around.

After the dust had cleared, Kirsten got up. She saw Scarlet lying on the ground, completely still. She called out to Matthew.

When he saw her, his instincts kicked in. He raced towards Scarlet's body. "Scarlet!" he cried. He knelt beside her body and wrapped his arms around her. "Scarlet? Scarlet! Wake up. Please, Scarlet. No. Don't do this to me. Scarlet, please ... wake up." Matthew's glasses clouded up. Seeing no sign of life on her face as she lay in his arms, he cried out. It was truly a heartbreaking moment. He felt as though his heart was shattering like delicate glass.

Matthew checked for a pulse again and again. But there was none. As the tears drenched his face, he held onto her and kissed her forehead. "I love you, Scarlet," he said. "I love you"

Afterlife

When Matthew and Kirsten got back to Washington DC, they informed Commander Rogers and Sergeant Fugeley that Scarlet had died for a heroic cause. Nothing about the darkness was ever mentioned. That was their secret to keep.

Kirsten was sent to notify Jennifer of Harry's death, while Matthew went to alert the Fendersons about Scarlet.

Before Matthew got out of his car, he stared at the house. He imagined how sad the family was about to be—about as sad as he was himself, he figured.

Finally, he exited the car and walked slowly to the front door. After he'd knocked a couple of times, Nicole opened the door. When she saw Matthew, she smiled. Then she asked about Scarlet. All he could do was shake his head. Her smile was replaced by sadness and grief; she collapsed into Matthew's arms.

George came out and looked at Matthew with a confused expression. All Matthew could do was shake is head.

Nicole slowly turned to her husband. "It's Scarlet," she said. She couldn't bear to finish the sentence; she collapsed in George's arms.

A tear trickled down George's cheek as he held his beloved wife in his arms.

"What's your name?" George asked, looking up at Matthew curiously.

"Matthew, sir, but my friends call me Matt," Matthew replied formally, holding back tears of his own.

George extended his left hand and placed it on Matthew's right shoulder. "You two were close," he said. He could tell Matthew was aching over the loss; his attempt to be stoic gave away his feelings for Scarlet. He could also see that Matthew was a good man. Though he was trying to hide his sadness, inside he'd always feel the heartache of Scarlet's loss as deeply as the Fendersons would.

———◆◆◈◆◆———

Over the next year, Matthew continued to grieve. He slipped into a depression that got worse every day. He rarely went out, his facial hair grew out, and he never forgot Scarlet. He was too afraid to forget.

What hurt him most was that he'd never actually told her that he loved her; this broke him more than her actual death.

Because he never forgot about Scarlet, he was afraid to move on. This hadn't happened after his two previous relationships, during his school and university years respectively, had ended. They had been nothing compared to his relationship with Scarlet. Their friendship had grown, and he had felt so comfortable with her.

Kirsten hadn't stopped grieving either. She relied on her girlfriend, Tanya, for support. But she kept waking up in the middle of the night in tears as she thought about Scarlet and the friendship they'd had.

At first, Kirsten had had a slight crush on Scarlet, but their friendship had grown. They had remained close. That's what really touched Kirsten. Other girls she'd known during her high school years had never truly befriended her once they had discovered she was gay. She had endured horrible teasing, hurtful comments, and the spreading of untrue rumours. But Scarlet had accepted Kirsten for who she was, and that was all Kirsten had ever wanted.

15 January 2018

The day of the funeral for Scarlet Daphne Jayden had been difficult for those who loved her.

The funeral was organised by the Fendersons, since they had legally adopted Scarlet as their own daughter. Matthew and Kirsten, along with Commander Rogers and Sergeant Fugeley had gotten involved as well.

George and Nicole offered had Matthew the opportunity to say a few things. He felt honoured and gladly accepted. They extended the same offer to Kirsten, Rogers, Fugeley, and Barnes, who had returned from Afghanistan shortly before Scarlet's death.

When Barnes heard the news, he was devastated. He'd been the one who had rescued Scarlet, along with Kirsten and Harry, from the Parwan detention facility. When he heard about Harry's earlier passing, he was shocked.

By the time they all got to the church, the time had struck 12.45 p.m. They were greeted by the Fendersons, along with their three grown children, Conner, Jodie, and Toby.

Soon everyone had arrived. Rita Holland, Liam's wife, was among the attendees. She had come on Liam's behalf.

When the vehicle carrying Scarlet's coffin arrived, tears streamed silently down Matthew's face, though he tried to remain straight-faced.

First, Pastor Clements came out to pay his respects and tell those who had gathered how things were gonna play out.

The pallbearers—Matthew, Kirsten, Commander Rogers, Sergeant Fugeley, Barnes, and Conner—lifted Scarlet's coffin. Matthew stared at it, and the tears flowed down his face, leaving his cheeks completely drenched.

As the music played, the pallbearers walked down the aisle. The music alone was enough make everyone cry as the coffin made its way down the aisle. Nicole completely lost it. She couldn't hold back the tears. She wept, pouring out the pain of her broken heart. George held his wife tightly in his arms, kissing her head gently as tears flowed down his cheeks.

As the ceremony went on, Matthew lost the will to cry anymore. He felt numb, even when he went to the front to give his speech. It felt like, as the words came out, he was struggling—trying with difficulty to speak out his feelings and thoughts.

"Scarlet Jayden was a brilliant friend with a troubled past," he said. "After she lost her brother when she was young, she faced a number of difficult obstacles. She became strong and tough and a true inspiration.

"Now my feelings for Scarlet were special, even though our relationship was cut short. I will always regret not telling her how much I loved her, which hurts more than ever."

After Matthew's speech, his words continued to echo in his mind. He thought about what he had said all the way to the cemetery. Matthew stood in the snowy graveyard until the end of the ceremony.

Standing over Scarlet's grave, he unclipped the rose broach from his jacket. Kneeling down, he held the broach to his lips, kissed it gently, and placed it on the tombstone. "I'll always love you, Scarlet," he whispered.

As he rose to his feet, a slight smile touched his lips, and a tear trickled down his cheek.

Now you see, life is as precious and delicate as glass. You never know what it'll throw at you. Whether good or bad, the decisions that will determine your life are yours to make. And if all seems to be going horribly wrong, and all you ever dream is that things will be "normal," then you're wrong. Life will never be normal. Life will continue to exist no matter what you do. As long as you stay strong and determined, you can accomplish fantastic things. You just have to ensure that you live life to the fullest for as long as you can hope and dream. Life will continue to test you no matter what.

Chapter 10b

Living

Survive

Just before I entered the house, Kirsten and Matthew took me aside. The devastation on the faces was more than enough to tell me how they felt about this.

First Kirsten came to me and wrapped her arms around me, tears filling her eyes. "Good luck, Scar. Promise me you'll try and make it out alive."

Kirsten's words hit me hard, as I couldn't make that promise. "Oh, Kirsten, you know I can't make a promise I'm not sure I can keep. I'm sorry," I replied.

She buried her face into my shoulder. That started the tears flowing from my eyes. I welcomed Kirsten's embrace.

Matthew had remained silent through Kirsten's goodbye. He'd simply watched on, scratching the back of his head down to his neck, his heart aching.

Kirsten gently kissed my forehead. Just then more of the dark attackers appeared. When Kirsten turned to engage them, Matthew stepped towards me.

"Do what you have to do," he said as he placed his hands on my arms.

I met his gaze, and we leaned into each other for one quick final kiss. The sensation felt out of place.

For Matthew, the chance to hold Scarlet was good. But it was also upsetting. He hadn't told her how he felt. If Scarlet died, he'd never get a chance to tell her he loved her.

No sooner had they stepped away from each other than one of the four-legged carnivores of darkness pounced on Matthew. Pinning him to the ground, it snarled and snapped. He grabbed his flashlight from his belt and shined it on the creature of darkness. Looking up, he saw that Scarlet was using her flashlight to help burn the creature off of him.

When he got up, he turned to her with resolve. Grabbing hold of his light firearm, he cried, "Go! We've got this."

With that, he dashed to Kirsten's side to help her fight more of the dark attackers.

The door, it seemed, was protected by darkness. I shined my light onto it, burning it away amid screams of agony.

As I entered, I could hear endless echoes of cries for help. "Let us go," the voices called. "Somebody help us. Let us go." I heard these words over and over again as I made my way up the stairs. I realised these voices belonged to the souls of her victims, who were being kept here by force instead of being at rest. I also realised I could hear Nathaniel's voice among them.

"I'm coming, big brother." I said quietly. "I'm here to set you free."

I searched the first few rooms for the mistress. One room in particular sparked a ton of memories. I had visions of playing together with Nathaniel and how he would never let me out of his sight. I recalled the banging on the door and the shouting that seemed endless. And I saw how he had vigilantly kept the door closed and the countless beatings he'd endured as a result.

As I exited the first bedroom, I made my way into the master bedroom across from the room I was in—the room where the mistress resided.

The moment I laid eyes on her, I thought I was in one of my dreams again. This moment felt terrifyingly surreal. When she spoke, I had to assimilate the new knowledge I had gained—this was the face of my mother, and that made sick to my stomach.

"At last we see one another, in person," she said as she slowly walked towards me. But before she could touch me, I pushed her back and pointed the flashlight at her. "Don't try it. You manipulated me before, but never again. You're finished," I said aggressively.

In response, she chuckled slightly, as the darkness sensed my anger.

She then blasted me to the wall, appearing in front of me in an instant flash of darkness. She lifted me up by the throat. "All that fear, now replaced by anger," she said coldly. "You know this would have ended long ago if you hadn't fought against me in your trials."

I tried to resist her harsh words.

It was then that we were interrupted by the wailing echoes of her victims and the brief hovering appearance of faces—images of souls kept in the darkness. Disturbed and horrified, I asked about the echoes.

She smiled slyly. "Most are my victims and previous faces I've worn over my years on this earth. I survive through nightmares and shadowed thoughts—like those of your poor weakling of a mother, who just wanted to never let you go after her second child died. Instead, she was branded dangerous and unstable."

"That's why Nathaniel sheltered me from her."

She slammed me against the wall, holding her face in front of mine. "That brother of yours was nothing more than an overprotective nosy little swine," she snarled.

After she said this, I had lost—my cheeks burned with the rage that was flaring up inside me. "Don't you dare say anything about my brother, you monster," I screamed. I kicked her with both legs, and she flew backwards into the master bedroom. Not bothering to catch the breath her tight grip had taken from me, I grabbed a flash bang from my belt. I hurled it at her as I leapt forward to grab the flashlight.

When the flash bang was about to explode, the mistress blasted it back towards me. Not only did this give me a massive headache, it also caused the floor all the way to the upstairs landing to crack and crumble to pieces.

Completely dazed from the blast, I couldn't get away from the crumbling floor in time. I fell along with it, landing belly first on some sort of coffee table.

The mistress leaned over and looked down from the doorway of the master bedroom. That sly smirk crossed her face, and then she shifted into a cloud of darkness and appeared right by me—almost as if she had quantum leaped.

I tried to get up, but she levitated me. I felt myself being pushed up and then held by thick clouds of darkness. Dark shackles attached to chains snapped around my wrists.

"So much anger and pretension." Her right hand had shifted and taken the form of a serrated machete blade. Slowly but gently, she caressed my cheeks with it. "You could be so much more, maybe even my new face."

As soon as she had spoken these words, I spat at her.

She levitated the fire poker and swung it across my mouth. I spat out blood on the floor as she chuckled, enjoying my pain.

"You don't scare me anymore," I said. My breath was rapid. I was in a great deal of pain and shock I was in.

I remembered the flares on my belt behind me. I carefully lifted my leg up, trying to lift one of the flares up and kick it free so I could catch it. I had to move quickly, as the darkness was making my hands ice cold. I could barely feel them.

Slowly I lifted the flare. And then finally, I managed to hurl it up along my right shoulder. I grabbed it with my mouth.

Noticing what I was doing, she shot towards me. But I hurled the flare to my right hand and worked my left arm over as rapidly as I could so I could light up the flare.

Once the flare popped, the light sparked brightly, burning the darkness that held me up. It also burned the mistress. She shrieked as the light scorched her skin and desperately moved away from me.

But once the flare died down, she released her rage upon me. She blasted me with darkness, levitated me, and then crashed me to the ground. I tried to reach for the flashlight, but she had me pinned. She went to drive her blade-like hand into me. I grabbed the blade with my bare hands, trying to keep it away from me. It sliced into my hands, and I could feel blood seeping from the gashes.

I brought my legs up and kicked the mistress away. She flew backwards, which gave me time to grab the flashlight finally. We both got to our feet at the same time.

I said Nathaniel's last words—"Be strong, little sis"—and then switched the flashlight on, just as the mistress fired her darkness. We collided. It was a fight to overpower one another. The darkness inside the house screeched in agonising pain. The pain of the darkness didn't help the mistress, but she fought through the pain.

As the light from the flashlight penetrated the darkness that had inhabited the house, the house began to fall apart; it had been left to nothing but rot and dust.

From above, a plank of wood that had been attached to one of the door frames snapped off and landed on my head, knocking me unconscious. But the flashlight was still switched on and continued to burn.

The mistress stumbled away from it, making her way towards me. She planned to use me as her next face.

———————◆◇◆◇◆———————

Kirsten and Matthew charged in, their firearms completely charged. They fired at the Mistress of Darkness, but the firearms didn't penetrate her like the flashlight did. Rather, the ammo stabbed into her like needles. So she blasted them with darkness.

Since Kirsten was up first, she used her last flash bang and then pulled out her flashlight. While she kept the mistress distracted, Matthew crawled over to Scarlet. He shook her arms, telling her to wake up.

———————◆◇◆◇◆———————

As I slowly regained consciousness, I winced. I was in a lot of pain and felt groggy. I found myself having difficulty trying to get my words out. "M ... M ... Matt?! What are Y ... you doing here?" I slowly opened my eyes.

"Even angels need angels, Miss Jayden." Matthew smiled. I could see in his eyes that he was relieved I was alive.

I smiled and then looked around for the mistress. To my surprise, I saw that Kirsten was keeping her distracted, fighting her with her flashlight.

Grabbing my flashlight, I turned to Matthew. "There's nothing you can do," I told him. "You need to get out of here."

I was about to face the mistress, but Matthew grabbed my arm and pulled me down towards him. "I know this is personal to you, Scar. But you don't have to face this alone," he said sternly, looking deeply into my eyes. I saw the concern in his eyes.

I knew I wouldn't have made it this far without Matthew and Kirsten. I realised I couldn't turn away from them. After all, during those trials I had saved their lives. Now, they were saving mine.

I decided to go along with Matthew. We managed to take cover by a ruined couch that had been tipped over backwards. It wasn't long before the mistress blasted Kirsten, throwing her back. She landed in front of us.

"Jesus holy Christmas cake Christ! That bitch is tough," Kirsten blurted out. Her head was pounding horribly from the blast and the hard landing.

The mistress then spun her arms around, creating a gust of wind made of darkness. Everything inside of the house was soon blowing everywhere. I was amazed that the house was still standing after all the abuse it had endured.

As the gust of darkness blew objects every which way, we remained hidden behind the couch. If we so much as peeked out behind the couch, we'd have to quickly duck back, narrowly escaping being whacked by some flying object.

"Got any bright ideas, Captain Scarlet?" Kirsten said sarcastically.

I was trying to figure out what we should do. I realised I still had a flash bang on my belt, and I tried to think of how I could combine it with my flashlight to fight back. When Matthew pulled out his bag and produced his last remaining flare, I had an idea. All we needed was duct tape. I told them about my plan.

"Wait!" Kirsten suddenly cried. "The light bombs have duct tape on them." She pulled her last light bomb from her belt.

She carefully pulled the duct tape off. Then Matthew and I held the flare and flash bang in place beside my flashlight, while Kirsten used the duct tape to wrap the three together.

We turned to face the mistress. I held the flashlight in a throwing position, my finger holding steady on the switch. Kirsten placed her left hand on the flare cap, and Matthew placed his right hand on the flash bang pin.

Once I said Nathaniel's last words for the final time, we stood up together. Kirsten pulled the cap off the flare. Matthew pulled the pin from the flash bang. And I switched on the flashlight. As they made a break for it, I hurled the flashlight towards the Mistress, who fired her darkness at me.

But the light pierced through the blast, devastating it. She screamed in agonising pain. I stood for a moment watching her, the way she had often watched me when I was in insufferable pain.

Then I made a run for it. The light continued to burn, and it was now flashing over and over, as if it was gonna explode. I jumped out through the glassless window and over the rotted picket fence, diving into Matthew's arms. We went down to the ground, bracing ourselves as the light made the darkness explode. It felt as if we were spat out from that dark realm and back into reality.

When I opened my eyes, I could see someone walking towards me. I released myself from Matthew's grip to see who it was.

When the figure got closer, I was completely stunned. "Mistress, you survived? … But how? Stay back!" I cried.

I was scared. I crawled backwards to get away from her. She didn't stop, and when she got a bit closer, it dawned on me that she wasn't wearing that black ballgown and veil over her face. Instead, she wore a light cream shirt and white jeans.

She knelt down next to me and placed her hands on my cheeks. And when I looked into her eyes, I knew who she was.

"My precious girl" Justine said, gently kissing my forehead.

She smiled at me one last time, and then William and Nathaniel appeared behind her. She turned, and her smiled widened as she got up and walked towards them.

It occurred to me that William must have been killed by the mistress not long after Matthew and I had left his run-down apartment. I felt torn up inside as I stared at him in shock.

While I watched on, tears flowed down my cheeks. Justine and William embraced each other. Then each took Nathaniel by the hand. Then the three of them turned to me and smiled—before walking into the light.

When reality finally caught up with me, I felt myself sobbing quietly. I had just seen my family disappear into a heavenly light.

It was then that Matthew and Kirsten, who'd been knocked out by the blast, finally got up and looked around, taking in that we were back on the empty lot. When they saw me, they ran towards me, calling out my name.

Still too shaken up to process all that had just happened, I didn't respond.

Matthew knelt beside me. He put his arm around me and rested his head on my head. I leaned my head into his chest, feeling a deep sadness as I took in that I was now the only Jayden alive.

But despite the pain and sorrow, there was something else. I was free from fear and darkness. So too had the souls of the previous victims and faces been set free from the darkness's clutches. They were laid to rest in peace like they should be. I knew they were smiling and saying, "Thank you."

Living

After we got back to Washington DC, I felt strange. Without the Mistress of Darkness's presence constantly stalking me, I finally felt free. Though I had dreamed of this day for so long, now that it was here, I was in shock. I was having a hard time processing that it was not a dream and not a nightmare. It was reality. In fact, it was a reality I had dreamed of for years. Not only was I free from the mistress, I had an adopted family who loved me as one of their own and friends who stuck by me no matter what.

Back at the base, I got myself checked over by the new junior medic who had taken over the position after Liam passed away. To my surprise, while I was getting patched up, Sergeant Fugeley came in and asked me to inform Harry's fiancée, Jennifer, of his passing.

As promised, the next morning Kirsten and I travelled to Boston, Massachusetts, to the Quincy area where Jennifer resided. As I stared at Jennifer's house, I kept imagining how her face would look when I told her he was gone. I felt so sad. Kirsten put her hand on my shoulder and gave me a comforting smile. Breathing out a long sigh, I got out of Kirsten's car, and Kirsten followed me to the door.

I knocked a couple of times. As we waited for her to open her door, the tension was killing me. I couldn't stop thinking about how broken-hearted she would be. Tears gathered in my eyes just imagining it.

Finally the door opened, and Jennifer said hello. She remembered Kirsten and me from that night at the welcome home ball.

When she asked where was Harry, neither of us could say a word. I just shook my head sadly, and Jennifer's smile disappeared, replaced by sorrow. She fell forward, and I caught her in my arms. As she sobbed into my shoulder, I cried along with her.

A few hours later, we left. We'd informed her Harry's funeral would be arranged by Commander Rogers and Sergeant Fugeley, and she's accepted the arrangement gratefully.

Back at the base, we were greeted by Matthew. I gratefully accepted his embrace. Kirsten, watching us, let out a slight giggled.

"I love you pair of lovebirds," she joked before walking to her apartment so she could get in touch with her girlfriend.

When she left, Matthew and I stared happily into each other's eyes. We were finally alone, without any threats of fear and death. It was, at last, time to accelerate our relationship. Holding each other, we shared a passionate kiss under the street lamps illuminating the car park and the romantic moonlight overhead.

15 January 2018

On a windy wintery afternoon at the Arlington National Cemetery, I stood beside Harry's grave, resting my head on Matthew's shoulder. Pastor Clements was saying some final words of goodbye on behalf of all of us who had gathered to share our sadness at his passing.

When we left, Jennifer remained at Harry's grave. It was clear she was still in shock at his death, struggling to come to terms with the situation and the reality that what they had planned together would never come true.

I walked back over to her, hoping to comfort her during this heartbreaking situation. I placed my hand on Jennifer's, but she was too numb to the world to notice at first. Even when I spoke some words of comfort she didn't seem aware I was there. "I'm really sorry, Jennifer. Harry was a great man and an excellent instructor," I said softly.

But Jennifer was unresponsive. She continued to stare at Harry's tombstone, too numb to cry anymore. I understood that, in this moment, she felt like nothing more than a shell—an empty shell.

26 April 2018

Some months had passed since the whole ordeal of the darkness had been put to rest. Matthew and I had been living our lives together. With the earnings we'd saved during our time with the CFA, we had bought an apartment together in Baltimore. That was where we wanted to live our life together. It might not be a normal life, but for me it would be a life of freedom, and that felt incredibly warming to me.

Every morning, between nine and ten, I would stand on the balcony watching the city down below and feeling the wind's gusts on my face and the sun's rays shining down on me. It was almost like Justine, William, and Nathaniel were looking down at me. And most days, a tear or two would trickle down my face as I imagined they were doing just that.

Matthew walked into the front room and saw his beautiful girlfriend standing on the balcony. Smiling with delight, he walked towards her. When she heard his footsteps, she turned to him. He wrapped his arms around her waist and rested his head on her shoulder. She covered his hand with hers and rested into him.

"They'd be proud of you, Scarlet," Matthew said.

"Yeah, yeah, I know they would be." She turned to Matthew, looking into his emerald green eyes as he looked into her sapphire blue eyes.

"I love you, Scar," Matthew said.

"I love you, Matt."

They both leaned into each other and shared a gentle, loving, passionate kiss.

Now not every life ends with a happy ending. It's the decisions in life that we choose for ourselves that determine that ending. Whether the outcome will be bad or good, we never know, as our future isn't written yet. There are still obstacles for us to overcome—no matter what, among them will be fear, death, victory, and sacrifice.

Each outcome you face comes from a decision you have made. And for the rest of your life, your decisions will mirror the type of person you are. Life is as precious and delicate as glass, and you never know what it'll throw at you.

If you think you can change your entire life so that you can act "normal"—the way you think everybody else around you is acting—then you're wrong. Life will never be normal. Life will continue to exist no matter what you do. As long as you stay strong and determined, you can accomplish fantastic goals. As long as you live life to the fullest, you can hope and dream. Life will test you no matter what—always.

Printed in Great Britain
by Amazon